unveiled

UNVEILED

Francine Rivers

TYNDALE HOUSE PUBLISHERS, INC.
WHEATON, ILLINOIS

Visit Tyndale's exciting Web site at www.tyndale.com

Check out the latest about Francine Rivers at www.francinerivers.com

Edited by Kathryn S. Olson

Designed by Julie Chen

Library of Congress Cataloging-in-Publication Data

Rivers, Francine, date
   Unveiled / Francine Rivers.
      p. cm. — (Lineage of grace)
   ISBN 0-8423-1947-6
   1. Tamar, daughter-in-law of Judah—Fiction.   2. Bible. O.T. Genesis—History of Biblical events—Fiction.   3. Women in the Bible—Fiction.   I. Title.

PS3568.I83165 U5 2000
813'.54—dc21   99-086431

Printed in the United States of America

06   05   04
9   8   7

To those who have been
abused and used and
yearn for justice.

I would like to thank

Ron Beers

for sharing his vision

Kathy Olson

for a fine job of editing

and the entire Tyndale team

for their continued support

And, as always, my gratitude to

Jane Jordan Browne

DEAR READER,

This is the first of five novellas on the women in the lineage of Jesus Christ. These were Eastern women who lived in ancient times, and yet their stories apply to our lives and the difficult issues we face in our world today. They were on the edge. They had courage. They took risks. They did the unexpected. They lived daring lives, and sometimes they made mistakes—big mistakes. These women were not perfect, and yet God in His infinite mercy used them in His perfect plan to bring forth the Christ, the Savior of the world.

We live in desperate, troubled times when millions seek answers. These women point the way. The lessons we can learn from them are as applicable today as when they lived thousands of years ago.

Tamar is a woman of **hope.**
Rahab is a woman of **faith.**
Ruth is a woman of **love.**
Bathsheba is a woman who received **unlimited grace.**
Mary is a woman of **obedience.**

These are historical women who actually lived. Their stories, as I have told them, are based on biblical accounts. Although some of their actions may seem disagreeable to us in our century, we need to consider these women in the context of their own times.

This is a work of historical fiction. The outline of the story is provided by the Bible, and I have started with the facts provided for us there. Building on that foundation, I have created action, dialogue, internal motivations, and in some cases, additional characters that I feel are consistent with the biblical record. I have attempted to remain true to the scriptural message in all points, adding only what is necessary to aid in our understanding of that message.

At the end of each novella, we have included a brief study section. The ultimate authority about people of the Bible is the Bible itself. I encourage you to read it for greater understanding. And I pray that as you read the Bible, you will become aware of the continuity, the consistency, and the confirmation of God's plan for the ages—a plan that includes you.

Francine Rivers

GENESIS 37:1–38:6

So Jacob settled again in the land of Canaan, where his father had lived.

This is the history of Jacob's family. When Joseph was seventeen years old, he often tended his father's flocks with his half brothers, the sons of his father's wives Bilhah and Zilpah. But Joseph reported to his father some of the bad things his brothers were doing. Now Jacob loved Joseph more than any of his other children because Joseph had been born to him in his old age. So one day he gave Joseph a special gift—a beautiful robe. But his brothers hated Joseph because of their father's partiality. They couldn't say a kind word to him.

One night Joseph had a dream and promptly reported the details to his brothers, causing them to hate him even more.

"Listen to this dream," he announced. "We were out in the field tying up bundles of grain. My bundle stood up, and then your bundles all gathered around and bowed low before it!"

"So you are going to be our king, are you?" his brothers taunted. And they hated him all the more for his dream and what he had said.

Then Joseph had another dream and told his brothers about it. "Listen to this dream," he said. "The sun, moon, and eleven stars bowed low before me!"

This time he told his father as well as his brothers, and his father rebuked him. "What do you mean?" his father asked. "Will your mother, your brothers, and I actually come and bow before you?" But while his brothers were jealous of Joseph, his father gave it some thought and wondered what it all meant.

Soon after this, Joseph's brothers went to pasture their father's flocks at Shechem. When they had been gone for some time, Jacob said to Joseph, "Your brothers are over at Shechem with the flocks. I'm going to send you to them."

"I'm ready to go," Joseph replied.

"Go and see how your brothers and the flocks are getting along," Jacob said. "Then come back and bring me word." So Jacob sent him on his way, and Joseph traveled to Shechem from his home in the valley of Hebron.

When he arrived there, a man noticed him wandering around the countryside. "What are you looking for?" he asked.

"For my brothers and their flocks," Joseph replied. "Have you seen them?"

"Yes," the man told him, "but they are no longer here. I heard your brothers say they were going to Dothan." So Joseph followed his brothers to Dothan and found them there.

When Joseph's brothers saw him coming, they recognized him in the distance and made plans to kill him. "Here comes that dreamer!" they exclaimed. "Come on, let's kill him and throw him into a deep pit. We can tell our father that a wild animal has eaten him. Then we'll see what becomes of all his dreams!"

But Reuben came to Joseph's rescue. "Let's not kill him," he said. "Why should we shed his blood? Let's just throw him alive into this pit here. That way he will die without our having to touch him." Reuben was secretly planning to help Joseph escape, and then he would bring him back to his father.

So when Joseph arrived, they pulled off his beautiful robe and threw him into the pit. This pit was normally used to store water, but it was empty at the time. Then, just as they were sitting down to eat, they noticed a caravan of camels in the distance coming toward them. It was a group of Ishmaelite traders taking spices, balm, and myrrh from Gilead to Egypt.

Judah said to the others, "What can we gain by killing our brother? That would just give us a guilty conscience. Let's sell Joseph to those Ishmaelite traders. Let's not be responsible for his death; after all, he is our brother!" And his brothers agreed. So when the traders came by, his brothers pulled Joseph out of the pit and sold him for twenty pieces of silver, and the Ishmaelite traders took him along to Egypt.

Some time later, Reuben returned to get Joseph out of the pit. When he discovered that Joseph was missing, he tore his clothes in anguish and frustration. Then he went back to his brothers and lamented, "The boy is gone! What can I do now?"

Then Joseph's brothers killed a goat and dipped the robe in its blood. They took the beautiful robe to their father and asked him to identify it. "We found this in the field," they told him. "It's Joseph's robe, isn't it?"

Their father recognized it at once. "Yes," he said, "it is my son's robe. A wild animal has attacked and eaten him. Surely Joseph has been torn in pieces!" Then Jacob tore his clothes and put on sackcloth. He mourned deeply for his son for many days. His family all tried to comfort him, but it was no use. "I will die in mourning for my son," he would say, and then begin to weep.

Meanwhile, in Egypt, the traders sold Joseph to Potiphar, an officer of Pharaoh, the king of Egypt. Potiphar was captain of the palace guard.

About this time, Judah left home and moved to Adullam, where he visited a man named Hirah. There he met a Canaanite woman, the daughter of Shua, and he married her. She became pregnant and had a son, and Judah named the boy Er. Then Judah's wife had another son, and she named him Onan. And when she had a third son, she named him Shelah. At the time of Shelah's birth, they were living at Kezib.

When his oldest son, Er, grew up, Judah arranged his marriage to a young woman named Tamar. . . .

WHEN Tamar saw Judah leading a donkey burdened with sacks and a fine rug, she took her hoe and ran to the farthest border of her father's land. Sick with dread, she worked with her back to the house, hoping he would pass by and seek some other girl for his son. When her nurse called her, Tamar pretended not to hear and hacked harder at the earth with her hoe. Tears blinded her.

"Tamar!" Acsah puffed as she reached her. "Didn't you see Judah? You must return to the house with me now. Your mother is about to send your brothers after you, and they'll not take kindly to your delay." Acsah grimaced. "Don't look at me like that, child. This isn't of my doing. Would you prefer a marriage with one of those Ishmaelite traders on his way to Egypt?"

"You've heard about Judah's son just as I have."

1

"I've heard." She held out her hand, and Tamar reluctantly relinquished the hoe. "Perhaps it will not be as bad as you think."

But Tamar saw in her nurse's eyes that Acsah had her own grave doubts.

Tamar's mother met them and grabbed Tamar by the arm. "If I had time, I would beat you for running off!" She pulled Tamar inside the house and into the women's quarters.

No sooner was Tamar through the doorway than her sisters laid hands upon her and tugged at her clothing. Tamar gasped in pain as one yanked the cover carelessly from her head, pulling her hair as well. "Stop it!" She raised her hands to ward them off, but her mother stepped in.

"Stand still, Tamar! Since it took Acsah so long to fetch you, we must hurry."

The girls were all talking at once, excited, eager.

"Mother, let me go just as I am!"

"Straight from the fields? You will not! You will be presented in the finest we have. Judah has brought gifts with him. And don't you dare shame us with tears, Tamar."

Swallowing convulsively, Tamar fought for self-control. She had no choice but to submit to her mother and sisters' ministrations. They were using the best garments and perfume for her appearance before Judah, the Hebrew. The man had three sons. If she pleased him, it would be the firstborn, Er, who would become her husband. Last harvest, when Judah and his sons had brought their flocks to graze in the harvested fields, her father had commanded her to work nearby. She knew what he hoped to accomplish. Now, it seemed he had.

"Mother, please. I need another year or two before I'm ready to enter a household of my own."

"Your father decides when you're old enough." Her mother wouldn't look her in the eyes. "It's not your right to question his judgment." Tamar's sisters chattered like magpies, making her want to scream. Her mother clapped her hands. "Enough! Help me get Tamar ready!"

Clenching her jaw, Tamar closed her eyes and decided she must resign herself to her fate. She had known that one day she would marry. She had also known her father would choose her husband. Her one solace was the ten-month betrothal period. At least she would have time to prepare her mind and heart for the life looming before her.

Acsah touched her shoulder. "Try to relax." She untied Tamar's hair and began to brush it with long, firm strokes. "Think soothing thoughts, dear one."

She felt like an animal her father was preparing for sale. Ah, wasn't she? Anger and despair filled her. Why did life have to be so cruel and unfair?

"Petra, bring the scented oil and rub her skin with it. She mustn't smell like a field slave!"

"Better if she smelled of sheep and goats," Acsah said. "The Hebrew would like that."

The girls laughed in spite of their mother's reprimand. "You're not making things better, Acsah. Now, hush!"

Tamar grasped her mother's skirt. "Please, Mother. Couldn't you speak to Father for my sake? This boy is . . . is evil!" Tears came in a rush before she could stop them. "Please, I don't want to marry Er."

Her mother's mouth jerked, but she did not weaken. She

pried Tamar's hand from the folds of her skirt and held it tightly between her own. "You know I can't alter your father's plans, Tamar. What good would come of my saying anything against this match now other than to bring shame upon us all? Judah is *here*."

Tamar drew in a ragged sob, fear flooding her veins.

Her mother gripped her chin and forced her head up. "I've prepared you for this day. You're of no use to us if you don't marry Er. See this for what it is: good fortune for your father's house. You will build a bridge between Zimran and Judah. We will have the assurance of peace."

"There are more of us than there are of them, Mother."

"Numbers don't always matter. You're no longer a child, Tamar. You have more courage than this."

"More courage than Father?"

Her mother's eyes darkened with anger. She released Tamar abruptly. "You will do as you're told or bear the full consequences of your disobedience."

Defeated, Tamar said no more. All she had done was to bring humiliation upon herself. She wanted to scream at her sisters to stop their silly prattling. How could they rejoice over her misfortune? What did it matter if Er was handsome? Hadn't they heard of his cruelty? Didn't they know of his arrogance? Er was said to cause trouble wherever he went!

"More kohl, Acsah. It will make her look older."

Tamar could not calm the wild beating of her heart. The palms of her hands grew damp. If all went as her father hoped, her future would be settled today.

This is a good thing, Tamar told herself, *a good thing.* Her throat was hot and tight with tears.

"Stand, Tamar," her mother said. "Let me have a look at you."

Tamar obeyed. Her mother sighed heavily and tugged at the folds of the red dress, redraping the front. "We must conceal her lack of curves, Acsah, or Zimran will be hard pressed to convince Judah she is old enough to conceive."

"I can show him the cloth, my lady."

"Good. Have it ready in case it's requested."

Tamar felt the heat flood her face. Was nothing private? Did everyone have to discuss the most personal events in her life? Her first show of blood had proclaimed her womanhood and her usefulness as a bargaining tool for her father. She was a commodity to be sold, a tool to forge an alliance between two clans, a sacrifice for an assured peace. She had hoped to be overlooked for another year or two. Fourteen seemed too young to draw a man's interest.

This is a good thing, Tamar told herself again. Even while other thoughts crowded in, tightening her stomach with fear, she repeated the words over and over, trying to convince herself. *This is a good thing.*

Perhaps if she hadn't heard the stories . . .

For as long as Tamar could remember, her father had been afraid of Judah and his people. She'd heard the stories about the power of the God of the Hebrews, a god who had turned Sodom and Gomorrah to rubble beneath a storm of fire and brimstone, leaving a wasteland of white sands and a growing salten sea behind. No Canaanite god had ever shown such power!

And there were the stories of what the Hebrews had done to the town of Shechem, stories of mayhem . . .

"Why must it be this way, Mother? Have I no choice in what's to become of me?"

"No more choice than any other girl. I know how you're feeling. I was no older than you when I came into your father's house. It is the way of things, Tamar. Haven't I prepared you for this day from the time you were a little girl? I have told you what you were born to do. Struggling against your fate is like wrestling the wind." She gripped Tamar's shoulders. "Be a good daughter and obey without quibbling. Be a good wife and bear many sons. Do these things, and you'll bring honor upon yourself. And if you're fortunate, your husband will come to love you. If not, your future will still be secure in the hands of sons. When you're old, they'll take care of you just as your brothers will take care of me. The only satisfaction a woman has in this life is knowing she has built up the household of her husband."

"But this is Judah's son, Mother. Judah's son Er."

Her mother's eyes flickered, but she remained firm. "Find a way to fulfill your duty and bear sons. You must be strong, Tamar. These people are fierce and unpredictable. And they are proud."

Tamar turned her face away. "I don't want to marry Er. I can't marry him—"

Her mother grasped her hair and yanked her head back. "Would you destroy our family by humiliating such a man as this Hebrew? Do you think your father would let you live if you went into that room and begged to be spared marriage to Er? Do you think Judah would take such an insult lightly? I tell you this. I would join your father in stoning you if you dare risk the lives of my sons. Do you hear me? Your father decides whom and when you marry. Not you!" She let go of her roughly and stepped away, trembling. "Do not act like a fool!"

Tamar closed her eyes. The silence in the room was heavy. She felt her sisters and nurse staring at her. "I'm sorry." Her lip quivered. "I'm sorry. I'll do what I must."

"As we all must." Sighing, her mother took her hand and rubbed it with scented oil. "Be wise as a serpent, Tamar. Judah has shown wisdom in considering you. You are strong, stronger than these others. You have quick wits and strength you don't even realize yet. This Hebrew has taken an interest in you. For all our sakes, you must please him. Be a good wife to his son. Build a bridge between our people. Keep the peace between us."

The weight of responsibility being given her made her bow her head. "I will try."

"You will do more than try. You will succeed." Her mother leaned down and kissed her cheek briskly. "Now sit quietly and collect yourself while I send word to your father that you're ready."

Tamar tried to think calmly. Judah was one of the sons of Jacob who had annihilated the town of Shechem over the rape of their sister. Perhaps, had the son of Hamor known more about these men, he would have left the girl alone. When he realized his mistake, he made every attempt to placate Jacob's sons. They wanted blood. The prince and his father had agreed to have every man in Shechem mutilated by the Hebrew rite of circumcision. They were desperate to bring about a marriage alliance and assurance of peace between the two tribes! They had done all the

Hebrews required, and still, three days after the Shechemites were circumcised, while they were all sick with fevers, Judah and his brothers took vengeance. They hadn't been content with the blood of the offender; they'd cut down every man by the sword. Not one survived, and the city was plundered.

Hebrews were a stench in Canaanite nostrils. Their presence invoked fear and distrust. Even though Judah had left his father's tent and come to live among Tamar's people, her father had never slept easily with Judah so close. Even Judah's longtime friendship with Hirah the Adullamite didn't reassure her father. Nor did it matter that Judah had taken a Canaanite wife, who had given him three sons and trained them up in Canaanite ways. Judah was Hebrew. Judah was a foreigner. Judah was a thorn in Zimran's side.

Over the years, her father had made contracts with Judah to bring flocks to his harvested fields. The arrangement had proven beneficial to everyone and had brought about a tentative alliance. All through those years, Tamar had known her father sought a better and more lasting way to keep peace between himself and the Hebrews. A marriage between the two households might ensure that if she succeeded in blessing Judah's household with sons.

Oh, Tamar understood her father's determination to bring about her marriage to Er. She even understood his need for it. She understood her role in all of it. But understanding didn't make it any easier. After all, she was the one being offered like a sacrificial lamb. She had no choice as to whether she married or not. She had no choice as to the man she would marry. Her only choice was in how she faced her fate.

Tamar was ready when her mother returned. Her feelings were hidden as she bowed down to her. When Tamar raised her head, her mother placed both hands upon her and murmured a blessing. Then she tipped Tamar's chin. "Life is difficult, Tamar. I know that better than you do. Every girl dreams of love when she's young, but this is life, not idle dreams. Had you been born first, we would have sent you to the temple of Timnah instead of your sister."

"I would not have been happy there." In fact, she would have preferred death by her own hand to the life her sister led.

"So this is the only life left to you, Tamar. Embrace it."

Resolved to do so, Tamar rose. She tried to still the tremors as she followed her mother from the women's chamber. Judah might still decide she was too young. He might say she was too skinny, too ugly. She might yet be spared from marrying Er. But it would change nothing in the end. The truth was hard to face. She had to marry, for a woman without a husband and sons might as well be dead.

+ + +

Judah watched Zimran's daughter closely as she entered the room. She was tall and thin and very young. She was also poised and graceful. He liked the way she moved as she served the meal with her mother. He'd noticed her youthful elegance during his last visit after the harvest. Zimran had put the girl to work in the field next to the pasturage so Judah and his sons could see her. He had been fully aware of Zimran's motives in displaying her this way. Now, on closer inspection, the girl looked too young to be a bride. She couldn't be more than Shelah's age, and Judah said so.

Zimran laughed. "Of course, she is young, but so much the better. A young girl is more moldable than an older one. Is that not so? Your son will be her *baal*. He will be her teacher."

"What of children?"

Zimran laughed again; the sound grated Judah's nerves. "I assure you, Judah my friend, Tamar is old enough to bear sons and has been old enough since last harvest, when Er noticed her. We have proof of it."

The girl's eyes flickered in her father's direction. She was blushing and clearly embarrassed. Judah felt oddly touched by her modesty and studied her openly. "Come closer, girl," he said, beckoning. He wanted to look into her eyes. Perhaps he would glean better understanding of why he'd thought of her at all when the subject of marriage had come to mind.

"Don't be shy, Tamar." Zimran's mouth flattened. "Let Judah see how pretty you are." When she raised her head, Zimran nodded. "That's it. Smile and show Judah what fine teeth you have."

Judah didn't care about her smile or her teeth, though both were good. He cared about her fertility. Of course, there was no way of knowing whether she could produce sons for his clan until she was wed to his son. Life held no guarantees. However, the girl came from good breeding stock. Her mother had produced six sons and five daughters. She must also be strong, for he had watched her in the fields hoeing the hard ground and carrying rocks to the wall. A weak girl would have been kept inside the house, making pottery or weaving.

"Tamar." Her father gestured. "Kneel before Judah. Let him have a closer look."

She obeyed without hesitation. Her eyes were dark but not hard, her skin ruddy and glowing with health. Such a girl might stir his son's hardened heart and make him repent of his wild ways. Judah wondered if she had the courage needed to gain Er's respect. Her father was a coward. Was she? Er had brought nothing but grief since he'd been old enough to walk, and he was likely to bring this girl trouble as well. She would have to be strong and resilient.

Judah knew the blame for Er's waywardness could be laid at his feet. He should never have given his wife a free hand in rearing his sons. He'd thought complete freedom would allow them to grow up happy and strong. Oh, they were happy as long as they got their way and were strong enough to abuse others if they didn't. They were proud and arrogant for lack of discipline. They would have turned out better had the rod been used more often!

Would this girl soften Er? Or would he harden and break her?

When she looked into his eyes, he saw innocence and intelligence. He felt a disquieting despair. Er was his first-born, the first show of the strength of his loins. He'd felt such pride and joy when the boy was born, such hope. *Ah,* he'd thought, *here is flesh of my flesh, bone of my bone!* How he'd laughed when the young sprout had stood in red-faced fury, refusing to obey his mother. He'd been amused by his son's passionate rebellion, foolishly proud of it. *This boy will be a strong man,* he'd said to himself. No woman would tell Er how to live.

Judah had never expected his son to defy *him* as well.

Onan, his second son, was becoming as difficult as Er. He'd grown up threatened by his older brother's white-hot jealousy and had learned to protect himself by cunning and deception. Judah didn't know which son was worse. Both were treacherous. Neither could be trusted.

The third son, Shelah, was following the ways of his brothers. Confronted with a wrong, Judah's sons lied or blamed others. When pressed hard enough to get the truth, they appealed to their mother, who defended them no matter how offensive their crimes. Her pride wouldn't allow her to see their faults. They were her sons, after all, and they were Canaanite through and through.

Something had to be done, or Er would bring Judah's head down to the ground in shame. Judah almost regretted having sons, for they wreaked havoc in his household and his life! There were moments when his rage was so intense, it was all he could do not to pick up a spear and hurl it at one of them.

Judah often thought about his father, Jacob, and the trouble *he'd* endured at the hands of *his* sons. Judah had caused his father as much trouble as the rest of them. Er and Onan reminded Judah of his brothers Simeon and Levi. Thinking of his brothers brought back the black memories of the grievous sin he himself had committed—the sin that haunted him, the sin that had driven him from his father's household because he couldn't bear to see the grief he'd caused or be in the company of the brothers who had shared in what he'd done.

His father, Jacob, didn't even know the full truth of what had happened at Dothan.

Judah tried to console himself. He'd kept Simeon and Levi from murdering their brother Joseph, hadn't he? But he also remembered that he was the one who'd led them into selling the boy to the Ishmaelite traders on their way to Egypt. He'd made a profit from the lad's misery—profits shared by his brothers as well. Only God knew if Joseph had survived the long, hard journey to Egypt. It was more than possible he'd died in the desert. If not, he was now a slave for some Egyptian.

Sometimes in the darkest hour of night, Judah would lie awake upon his pallet, filled with an agony of remorse, thinking about Joseph. How many years would it be before he could put the past behind him and forget what he'd done? How many years before he could close his eyes and not see Joseph's hands shackled, his neck noosed, as he was led forcefully away by the Ishmaelite traders? The boy's screams for help still echoed in Judah's mind.

He had the rest of his life to regret his sins, years to live with them. Sometimes Judah swore he could feel the hand of God squeezing the life from him for plotting the destruction of his own brother.

Zimran cleared his throat. Judah reminded himself where he was and why he'd come to the home of this Canaanite. He mustn't let his mind wander, mustn't allow the past to intrude on what he had to do about the future. His son needed a wife—a young, comely, strong wife who might distract him from his wicked schemes and devices. Judah's mouth tightened as he studied the Canaanite girl kneeling before him. Was he making another mistake? He'd married a Canaanite and lived to regret it. Now he was bringing another one into his household. Yet this Canaanite girl appealed to him. Why?

Judah tipped the girl's chin. He knew she must be afraid, but she hid it well. That would be a useful skill where Er was concerned. She looked so young and guileless. Would his son destroy her innocence and corrupt her as he was so eager to do to others?

Hardening himself, Judah withdrew his hand and leaned back. He had no intention of allowing Er to make the same mistakes he had. Lust had driven him to marry the boy's mother. Beauty was a snare that captured a man, while unrestrained passion burned away reason. A woman's character mattered greatly in a marriage. Judah would have done better to follow custom and allow his father to choose a wife for him. Instead, he'd been stubborn and hasty and now suffered for his folly.

It wasn't enough that a woman stirred a man's passion. She also had to be strong, yet willing to bend. A stubborn woman was a curse upon a man. He'd been laughable in his youthful confidence, so certain he could bend a woman to his ways. Instead, he'd bent to Bathshua's. He'd fooled himself into thinking there was no harm in giving his wife freedom to worship as she wished. Now, he found himself reaping a whirlwind with his idol-worshiping sons! wife's fault.

Tamar was of calmer disposition than Bathshua. Tamar had courage. She appeared intelligent. He knew she was strong, for he'd watched how hard she worked. His wife, Bathshua, would be happy about that. No doubt she would dump her chores upon the girl as soon as possible. The quality that mattered most was her fertility, and only time would tell about that. The qualities he could see were more than enough. Yet there was something more about this girl that Judah couldn't define—something rare and wonderful that made him determined to have her in his family. It was as though a quiet voice was telling him to choose her.

"She pleases me."

Zimran exhaled. "You are a wise man!" He nodded to his daughter. Thus dismissed, Tamar rose. The Canaanite was clearly eager to begin negotiations. Judah watched the girl leave the room with her mother. Zimran clapped his hands; two servants hurried in, one with a tray of pomegranates and grapes, another with roasted lamb. "Eat, my brother, and then we will talk."

Judah would not be so easily manipulated. Before touching the food, he made an offer for the girl. Eyes glowing, Zimran plunged in and began haggling over the bride-price.

Judah decided to be generous. Marriage, though far from bringing happiness to him, had brought some stability and direction. Perhaps Er would be similarly diverted from riotous living. Besides, Judah wanted to spend as little time with Zimran as possible. The man's ingratiating manner irritated him.

Tamar. Her name meant "date palm." It was a name given to one who would become beautiful and graceful. A date palm survives the desert and bears sweet, nourishing fruit, and the girl came from a fertile family. A date palm sways in the desert winds without breaking or being uprooted, and this girl would have to face Er's quick, irascible temper. A date palm could survive a hostile environment, and Judah knew Bathshua would see this young girl as her

15

rival. Judah knew his wife would pit herself against this young bride because Bathshua was vain and jealous of her son's affections.

Tamar.

Judah hoped the girl held all the promise her name implied.

✦　✦　✦

Tamar waited while her fate was settled. When her mother stood in the doorway, she knew the matter of her future was decided. "Come, Tamar. Judah has gifts for you."

She rose, numb inside. It was a time for rejoicing, not tears. Her father need not fear any longer.

"Ah, Daughter." Her father smiled broadly. Obviously, he'd fetched a high bride-price for her, for he had never before embraced her with so much affection. He even kissed her cheek! She lifted her chin and looked into his eyes, wanting him to know what he'd done to her in giving her to such a man as Er. Perhaps he would feel some shame for using her to protect himself.

He didn't. "Greet your father-in-law."

Resigned to her fate, Tamar prostrated herself before Judah. The Hebrew put his hand upon her head and blessed her and bid her rise. As she did so, he took gold earrings and bracelets from a pouch at his waist and placed them upon her. Her father's eyes glowed, but her heart sank.

"Be ready to leave in the morning," Judah told her.

Shocked, she spoke without thinking. "In the morning?" She looked at her father. "What of the betrothal—?"

Her father's expression warned her to silence. "Judah and I celebrate tonight, my daughter. Acsah will pack your things and go with you tomorrow. Everything is settled. Your husband is eager for you."

Was her father so afraid that he didn't require the customary ten-month betrothal period to prepare for the wedding? She would not even have a week to adjust to her impending marriage!

"You may go, Tamar. Make ready to leave in the morning."

When she entered the women's chamber, she found her mother and sisters already packing for her. Unable to contain her feelings any longer, Tamar burst into tears. Inconsolable, she wept all night, even after her sisters whined and pleaded for her to stop. "You will have your day," she told them angrily. "Someday you will understand!"

Acsah held and rocked her, and Tamar clung to her childhood for one last night.

When the sun rose, she washed her face and donned her bridal veils.

Her mother came to her. "Be content, beloved one. Judah paid dearly for you." Her voice was tear-choked and faintly bitter. "That Hebrew came with a donkey laden with gifts. He returns home with only his seal ring and staff."

"And me," Tamar said softly.

Her mother's eyes filled with tears. "Take good care of her, Acsah."

"I will, my lady."

Her mother took Tamar in her arms and kissed her. "May your husband love you and give you many sons," she whispered against her hair. Tamar clung to her tightly, pressing herself close, soaking in the warmth and softness of her mother one last time. "It's time," her mother said softly, and

Tamar drew back. Her mother touched her cheek before turning away.

Tamar went out into the morning sunlight. Acsah walked with her as she headed toward her father and Judah, who were standing some distance away. She had cried herself out last night. She would shed no more childish tears, though it was hard not to do so with Acsah weeping softly behind her.

"Perhaps all we've heard isn't true," Acsah said. "Perhaps Er is not as bad as some say he is."

"What does it matter now?"

"You must try to make him love you, Tamar. A man in love is clay in a woman's hands. May the gods have mercy on us!"

"Have mercy upon me and be quiet!"

When she reached the two men, her father kissed her. "Be fruitful and multiply the household of Judah." He was eager for their departure.

Judah walked ahead, Tamar and Acsah following. He was a tall man with long strides, and Tamar had to walk quickly to keep up with him. Acsah muttered complaints under her breath, but Tamar paid her no attention. Instead, she set her mind on what lay ahead. She would work hard. She would be a good wife. She would do everything within her power to bring honor to her husband. She knew how to plant a garden, tend a herd, cook, weave, and make pottery. She could read and write enough to keep proper lists and records of household goods. She knew how to conserve food and water when times were bad and how to be generous when times were good. She knew how to make soap, baskets, cloth, and tools, as well as how to organize servants. But children would be the greatest blessing she could give her husband—children to build the household.

It was Judah's second son, Onan, who came out to meet them. "Er is gone," he said to his father while staring at her.

Judah slammed the end of his staff into the ground. "Gone where?"

Onan shrugged. "Off with his friends. He was angry when he heard where you'd gone. I stayed out of his way. You know how he gets."

"Bathshua!" Judah strode toward his stone house.

A buxom woman with heavily painted eyes appeared in the doorway. "What are you yelling about this time?"

"Did you tell Er I was bringing his bride home today?"

"I told him." She leaned indolently in the doorway.

"Then where is he?"

She lifted her chin. "I'm his mother, Judah, not his keeper. Er will be along when he's ready and not before. You know how he is."

Judah's face darkened. "Yes, I know how he is." He gripped his staff so tightly his knuckles turned white. "That's why he needs a wife!"

"That may be, Judah, but you said the girl was pretty." She gave Tamar a cursory glance. "Do you really think this skinny girl will turn Er's head?"

"Tamar is more than she seems. Show her to Er's chamber." Judah walked off, leaving Tamar and Acsah standing before the house.

Mouth tight, Bathshua looked Tamar over from head to foot. She shook her head in disgust. "I wonder what Judah was thinking when he chose you?" Turning her back, she went into the house and left Tamar and Acsah to fend for themselves.

✦   ✦   ✦

Er returned late in the afternoon, accompanied by several Canaanite friends. They were drunk and laughing loudly. Tamar remained out of sight, knowing what men were like in this condition. Her father and brothers had often imbibed freely and argued violently because of it. She knew the wisdom of staying out of the way until the effects of the wine wore off.

Knowing she would be summoned, Tamar had Acsah array her in wedding finery. While waiting, Tamar willed herself to set aside every terrible thing she'd ever heard about Er. Perhaps those who had spoken against him had hidden motives. She would give him the respect due a husband and adapt herself to his demands. If the god of his father smiled upon her, she would give Er sons, and quickly. If she were so blessed, she would bring them up to be strong and honest. She would teach them to be dependable and loyal. And if Er so wished, she would learn about the God of Judah and bring up her sons to worship him rather than bow down to the gods of her father. Still, her heart trembled and her fears increased with each passing hour.

When Tamar was finally summoned and saw her husband, she felt a flicker of admiration. Er was tall like his father and held the promise of great physical strength. He had his mother's thick curling mass of black hair, which he had drawn back in Canaanite fashion. The brass band he wore around his forehead made him look like a young Canaanite prince. Tamar was awed by her husband's handsome appearance but filled quickly with misgivings when she looked into his eyes. They were cold and dark and devoid of mercy. There was pride in the tilt of his head, cruelty in the curve of his lips, and indifference in his manner. He didn't reach out to take her hand.

"So this is the wife you chose for me, Father."

Tamar shivered at his tone.

Judah put his hand firmly on his son's shoulder. "Take good care of what belongs to you, and may the God of Abraham give you many sons by this girl."

Er stood unblinking, his face an inscrutable mask.

All through the evening, Er's friends made crude jests about marriage. They teased Er unmercifully, and though he laughed, Tamar knew he wasn't amused. Her father-in-law, lost in his own thoughts, drank freely while Bathshua lounged nearby, eating the best tidbits of the wedding feast and ignoring her. Tamar was hurt and confused and embarrassed by such rudeness. What had she done to offend her mother-in-law? It was as though the woman was determined not to show her the least consideration.

As the night wore on, her fear gave way to depression. She felt abandoned and lost in the midst of the gathering. She had married the heir of Judah's household, and yet no one spoke to her, not even the young husband who sat beside her. The hours passed slowly. She was bone weary from lack of sleep the previous night and the long walk to her new home. The tensions of the wedding feast further sapped her. She fought to keep her eyes open. She fought even harder to keep the tears from welling up and spilling over.

Er pinched her. Tamar gasped and jerked away from him. Heat flooded her cheeks as she realized she had unwittingly dozed against his side. His friends were laughing and making jokes about her youth and the impending wedding night. Er laughed with them. "Your nurse has prepared the chamber for us." He took her hand and pulled her up to her feet.

As soon as Acsah closed the door of the bedchamber behind them, Er stepped away from Tamar. Acsah took her place outside the door and began singing and beating her small drum. Tamar's skin prickled. "I'm sorry I fell asleep, my lord."

Er said nothing. She waited, her nerves stretching taut. He was enjoying her tension, plucking her nerve endings with his silence. Folding her hands, she decided to wait him out. He removed his belt sardonically. "I noticed you last year when we brought the sheep to your father's fields. I suppose that's why my father thought you might do as my wife." His gaze moved down over her. "He doesn't know me very well."

She did not fault Er for the hurtful words. She felt he was justified. After all, her heart had not leapt with joy when Judah came and offered a bride-price for her.

"You're afraid of me, aren't you?"

If she said no, it would be a lie. To say yes would be unwise.

His brow rose. "You should be afraid. I'm angry, or can't you tell?"

22

She could, indeed, and couldn't guess what he would do about it. She remained silent, acquiescent. She'd seen her father in rages often enough to know that it was better to say nothing. Words were like oil on a fiery temper. Her mother had told her long ago that men were unpredictable and given to fits of violence when provoked. She would not provoke Er.

"Cautious little thing, aren't you?" He smiled slowly. "At least you keep your wits about you." He came toward her. "You've heard things about me, I'll bet." He brushed his fingers against her cheek. She tried not to flinch. "Have your brothers carried stories home?"

Her heart beat faster and faster.

"As my father said, you're mine now. My own little mouse to do with as I wish. Remind me to thank him." He tipped her chin. His eyes glittered coldly, reminding her of a jackal in the moonlight. When he leaned down and kissed her mouth, the hair on the back of her neck rose. He drew back, assessing her. "Believe the rumors, every one of them!"

"I will try to please you, my husband." Heat poured into her cheeks at the quaver in her voice.

"Oh, no doubt you will try, my sweet, but you won't succeed." His mouth curved, showing the edge of his teeth. "You can't."

It took only a day of the weeklong wedding celebration for Tamar to understand what he meant.

two

TAMAR tensed as she heard Er shouting inside the house. Bathshua was shouting back at him. Even with the midday sun beating down upon Tamar's back, her sweat turned cold. Judah had summoned his eldest son to assist with the flocks, but it seemed Er had plans of his own. Er's temper was hot enough now that he would seek out some way to vent it, and his wife would be an easy target. After all, no one would interfere.

Keeping her head down, Tamar continued hoeing the rocky patch of soil Bathshua had assigned to her care. She wished she could shrink to the size of an ant and scurry down a hole. Inside the house, the ranting of son and raving of mother continued. Tamar knelt once, fighting against frightened tears as she pried a large rock from the ground. Straightening, she tossed it toward the growing pile nearby.

In her mind she built a wall around herself, high and thick, with a clear sky above. She didn't want to think about Er's temper and what he might do to her this time.

"She's losing her hold on him," Acsah said grimly as she worked a few feet away.

"It does no good to worry, Acsah." The words were uttered more to remind herself than Acsah. Tamar kept working. What else could she do? Four months in Judah's house had taught her to avoid her husband whenever possible, especially when he was in a bad temper. She'd also learned to hide her fear. Her heart might race with it, her stomach be tight as a knot, her skin cold and clammy, but she dared not reveal her feelings, for Er relished fear. He fed upon it.

"A pity Judah isn't here." Acsah made a sound of disgust. "Of course, he's never here." She hit the hard ground with her hoe. "Not that he can be blamed."

Tamar said nothing. Her mind worked frantically, searching for an escape and finding none. If only Judah hadn't gone ahead. If only he'd taken Er with him in the first place, rather than send a servant back later to fetch him. When Judah was present, Er could be managed. When he was absent, Er ran wild. The chaos of this family came from Judah's failure to exercise his authority often enough. Judah preferred the open spaces of hills and fields to the confines of his house. Tamar didn't fault him—sheep and goats were peaceful, complacent company compared to a contentious wife and hot-tempered, quarrelsome sons. Sometimes Er and Onan behaved like wild beasts tied together and thrown into a box!

Judah could run away from unpleasantness. Judah could hide from responsibility. Tamar had to live with danger day after day.

Her body jerked as something large crashed inside the house. Bathshua screamed tearful curses down upon her son. Er retaliated. More crockery hit the wall. A metal cup flew out the doorway and bounced across the ground.

"You must stay away from the house today," Acsah said quietly.

"Bathshua may prevail." Turning away, Tamar gazed toward the distant hills while the battle raged behind her. Her hand trembled as she wiped the perspiration from her face. Closing her eyes, she sighed. Perhaps Judah's command would be enough this time.

"Bathshua always prevails in one way or another," Acsah said bitterly. She scraped angrily at the dry earth. "If screaming fails, she'll sulk until she gets her way."

Tamar ignored Acsah and tried to think of more pleasant things. She thought of her sisters. They had squabbles, but they enjoyed one another's company. She remembered how they had sung together as they worked and told stories to entertain one another. Her father had a temper like any other man, and there had been loud arguments at times between her brothers, but nothing in her experience had prepared her for Judah's household. Each day she tried to arise with new hope, only to have it crushed again.

"If only I had a place here, Acsah, some small corner of influence . . ." She spoke without self-pity.

"You will have when you produce a son."

"A son." Tamar's heart ached with longing. She longed for a child more than anyone, even her husband, whose desire for a son was more an extension of his own pride than a desire to prosper his family. For Tamar, a son would secure her position in the household. She would no longer feel such loneliness, with a baby in her arms. She could love a son and hold him close and receive love from him. Perhaps a son would even soften Er's heart toward her— and his hand as well.

She remembered again Bathshua's crushing condemnation: "If you didn't disappoint my son, he wouldn't beat you so often! Do as he wishes, and perhaps he will treat you better!" Tamar blinked back tears, fighting against self-pity. What good would that do? It would only weaken her resolve. She was a member of this family, whether she wanted to be or not. She mustn't allow her emotions to prevail. She knew Bathshua delighted in making hurtful remarks. A day never passed without her mother-in-law's finding some way to stab at her heart.

"Another moon has passed, Tamar, and *still* you haven't conceived! I was with child a week after I wed Judah!"

Tamar could say nothing without rousing Er's temper. What defense had she when nothing she did pleased her mother-in-law or her young husband? She ceased to hope for tenderness or compassion from either of them. Honor and loyalty seemed to be missing as well, for Bathshua had to resort to threats to get Er to obey Judah's summons.

"Enough, I say!" Er shouted in frustration, drawing Tamar's attention back to the altercation between mother and son. *"Enough!* I'll go to Father! Anything to get away from your carping!" He stormed out of the house. *"I hate sheep!* If I had my way, I'd *butcher every one of them!"*

Bathshua appeared in the doorway, arms akimbo, chest heaving. "And then what would you have? Nothing!"

"I'd have the money from their meat and hides. That's what I'd have."

"All of which you'd spend in a week. Then what? Have I raised such a fool?"

Er called her a name and made a rude gesture at her before turning and striding away. Tamar held her breath until she saw he was taking the path away from Kezib. She would have a few days' respite from his cruelty.

"It seems Bathshua won this battle," Acsah said. "But there will be another, and another," she added dismally.

Lighter of heart, Tamar smiled and returned to her work. "Each day has trouble enough, Acsah. I'll not burden myself with worrying about tomorrow."

"Tamar!" Bathshua stepped outside. "If you have time enough for idle chatter, you can come clean up this mess!" Swinging around, she marched back into the house.

"She expects you to clear up the destruction she and Er have made of that house," Acsah said with loathing.

"Hush, or you'll bring more trouble upon us."

Bathshua appeared again. "Leave Acsah to finish in the garden. I want you inside this house *now!"* She disappeared inside.

When Tamar entered the house, she treaded carefully so that she wouldn't step on the shards of broken pottery strewn across the earthen floor. Bathshua sat glumly staring at her broken loom. Hunkering down, Tamar began to gather the shards of a jug into the folds of her *tsaiph*.

"I hope Judah is satisfied with the mess he's made," Bathshua said angrily. "He thought a wife would improve Er's disposition!" She glared at Tamar as though she were to blame for everything that had happened. "Er is worse than ever! You've done my son more harm than good!"

Fighting tears, Tamar made no defense.

Muttering imprecations, Bathshua tipped the loom up. Seeing that the arm was broken and the rug she'd made tangled, she covered her face and wept bitterly.

Tamar was embarrassed by the woman's passion. It wasn't the first time she'd seen Bathshua burst into tempestuous tears. The first time, she'd gone to her mother-in-law and tried to comfort her, only to receive a resounding slap across the face and blame for the woman's despair. Tamar kept her distance now and averted her eyes.

Was Bathshua blind to what she caused in this household? She constantly pitted son against father and son against son. She argued with Judah over everything—and in front of her sons—teaching them to rebel and follow their own desires rather than do what was best for the family. It was no wonder her mother-in-law was miserable! And everyone was miserable right along with her.

"Judah wants Er to tend the sheep." Bathshua yanked at the loom, making a worse mess. "You know why? Because my husband can't bear to be away from his *abba* for more than a year! He has to go back and see how that wretched old man is doing. You watch when Judah comes home. He'll brood for days. He won't speak to anyone. He won't eat.

Then he'll get drunk and say the same stupid thing he does every time he sees Jacob." She grimaced as she mocked her husband. "'The hand of God is upon me!'"

Tamar glanced up.

Bathshua rose and paced. "How can the man be such a fool—believing in a god who doesn't even exist?"

"Perhaps he does exist."

Bathshua cast a baleful glance at her. "Then where is he? Has this god a temple in which to live or priests to serve him? He doesn't even have a *tent!*" Her chin tipped in pride. "He's not like the gods of Canaan." She marched to her cabinet and flung it open. "He is not a god like *these.*" She held her hand out toward her teraphim reverently. "He isn't a god you can see." She ran her hand down one statue. "He isn't a god you can touch. These gods fan our passions into being and make our land and our women fertile." Her eyes glittered coldly. "Perhaps if you were more respectful to them, you wouldn't still have a flat, empty belly!"

Tamar felt the barb, but this time she didn't allow it to sink in deeply. "Didn't the God of Judah destroy Sodom and Gomorrah?"

Bathshua laughed derisively. "So some say, but I don't believe it." She closed the cabinet firmly, as though such words would bring bad luck upon her house. She turned and frowned down upon Tamar. "Would you raise up your sons to bow down to a god who destroys cities?"

"If Judah wills it."

"Judah," Bathshua said and shook her head. "Have you ever seen my husband worship his father's god? I never have. So why should his sons or I worship him? You will train up your sons in the religion of Er's choice. I have never bowed down to an unseen god. Not once have I been unfaithful to the gods of Canaan, and I advise you to be faithful as well. If you know what's good for you . . ."

Tamar recognized the threat.

Bathshua sat upon a cushion against the wall and smiled coldly. "Er wouldn't be pleased to hear you were even thinking of worshiping the god of the Hebrews." Her eyes narrowed. "I think you're the cause of our troubles."

Tamar knew what to expect. When Er returned, Bathshua would claim there was spiritual insurrection in the household. The woman relished stirring up trouble. Tamar longed to throw the broken crockery on the earthen floor and tell her mother-in-law it was her own actions that were destroying the family. Instead, she swallowed her anger and collected shards as Bathshua watched.

"The gods have blessed me with three fine sons, and I've brought them up in the *true* religion, as would any *good* mother."

Hot-tempered sons, who do even less work than you do, Tamar wanted to say but held her tongue. She couldn't win a war with her mother-in-law.

Bathshua leaned forward and lifted an overturned tray enough to pluck a bunch of grapes. She dropped the tray again. "Perhaps you should pray to Asherah more often and give better offerings to Baal. Then your womb might be opened."

Tamar lifted her head. "I know of Asherah and Baal. My father and mother gave up my sister to serve as a priestess in the temple of Timnah." She didn't add that she'd never been able to embrace their beliefs or say aloud that she pitied her sister above all women. Once, during a visit to Timnah during a festival, she'd seen her older sister on an altar platform having sexual intercourse with a priest. The rites were intended to arouse Baal and bring spring back to the land, but Tamar had been filled with disgust and fear at what she saw, sickened even more by the excited crowd witnessing the scene. She'd drawn back, ducked around the corner of a building, and run away. She hadn't stopped running until she was out of Timnah. She'd hidden in the middle of an olive orchard and remained there until evening when her mother found her.

"You are not devout enough," Bathshua said smugly.

No, I am not, Tamar said to herself. She knew she could never be devout when she didn't believe. The gods made no sense to her. All her efforts to worship them filled her with a strange sense of repugnance and shame.

Bathshua rose and returned to her loom. She had calmed enough to begin straightening the tangled threads. "If you were a true believer, you'd be with child by now." She glanced at Tamar, no doubt trying to assess the impact of her mean-spirited words. "It would seem the gods are angry with you, wouldn't it?"

"Perhaps," Tamar conceded with a pang of guilt. Bathshua's teraphim were nothing but clay, stone, and wood statues. She couldn't embrace them as Bathshua did, nor could she adore them as fervently. Oh, Tamar said the prayers expected of her, but the words were empty and held no power. Her heart was untouched, her mind far from convinced.

If the gods of Canaan were so powerful, why hadn't they been able to save or protect the people of Sodom and Gomorrah? Surely a dozen gods were more powerful than one—if they were true gods.

They were nothing but carved stone, chipped wood, and clay molded by human hands!

Perhaps there was no true god.

Her heart rebelled at this thought as well. The world around her—the heavens, the earth, the winds, and the rain—said there was something. Perhaps the God of Judah was that *something*. A shield against enemies. A shelter in a storm. Nay, a fortress . . . oh, how she longed to know. Yet she dared not ask.

What right had she to bother Judah with questions, especially when so many other things plagued him?

Someday, perhaps, she would have the time and the opportunity to ask.

In the meantime, she would wait and hope to see some sign of what Judah believed and how he worshiped.

✦   ✦   ✦

Judah and Er returned five days later. Tamar heard them arguing long before they entered the house. So did Bathshua, for she sighed heavily. "Go and milk one of the goats, Tamar, and tell your nurse to make some bread. Perhaps if the men eat, they will be in better humor."

By the time Tamar returned with a jug of fresh goat's milk, Judah was reclining against some cushions. His eyes were closed, but Tamar knew he wasn't asleep. His face was tense, and Bathshua was sitting close by, glaring at him.

She'd probably been vexing him again, and he was doing his best to shut her out.

"Five days, Judah. *Five days.* Did you have to stay that long?"

"You could have come with me."

"And done what? Listen to your brothers' wives? What have I in common with them? And your mother doesn't like me!" She whined and complained like a selfish child.

Tamar offered Er milk. "Wine," he said with a jerk of his chin, clearly in a surly mood. "I want wine!"

"I'll have milk," Judah said, his eyes opening enough to look at her.

Bathshua's head came up. "Here! Give me that. I'll serve my husband while you see to my son." When she had the jug, she sloshed some milk into a cup, thrust it at Judah, and then set the jug within his reach so that he could serve himself next time.

Bathshua was still badgering Judah when Tamar returned with wine for Er.

"What good does it do you to see your father, Judah? Has anything changed? You're always miserable when you come home from his tent. Let Jacob grieve over his second wife and son. Forget about him. Every time you go back to see him, you come home and make my life miserable!"

"I will not forsake my father," Judah said, his jaw clenched.

"Why not? He's forsaken you. A pity the old man doesn't die and spare us all. . . ."

"Enough!" Judah roared. Tamar saw that it was not anger but pain that made him cry out. Grimacing, he raked his

hands back through his hair. "Just once, Bathshua, hold your tongue!" He raised his head and glared at her. "Even better, leave me alone!"

"How can you speak to me so cruelly?" She wept angrily. "I'm the mother of your sons. *Three* sons!"

"Three worthless sons." Judah's eyes narrowed coldly on Er.

Tamar's stomach dropped as she waited for him to say something that would rouse Er's temper. Her husband would control his temper as long as he was in his father's presence, but later she would be the recipient of his frustration. Bathshua kept on until Tamar wanted to scream at her to stop, to leave, to have some particle of common sense. Thankfully, Bathshua stormed out of the room, leaving silence behind her.

Tamar was left alone to serve both men. The tension in the room made her nerves tingle. She replenished Er's cup of wine. He emptied the cup and held it out for more. She glanced at Judah before refilling it. Er looked up at her with a scowl, then at his father. "Onan and Shelah can see to the flocks for the next few days. I'm going to see my friends."

Judah raised his head slowly and looked at his son. "Will you?" His voice was soft, his eyes hard.

Er shifted. He looked into his cup and then drained it. "With your permission, of course."

Judah gazed at Tamar and then looked away. "Go ahead. But stay out of trouble this time."

A muscle jerked in Er's cheek. "I never start trouble."

"Of course not," Judah said drolly.

Er stood and approached Tamar. She drew back instinctively, but he caught hold of her arm and pulled her close. "I'll miss you, my sweet." His expression mocked his words, and his fingers bit into her flesh. He let go of her and pinched her cheek. "Don't pine. I won't be gone long!"

Judah sighed with relief when his son was gone. He scarcely noticed Tamar's presence. Leaning forward, he held his head as though it ached. Tamar hunkered down quietly and waited for him to command her to leave. He didn't. When Acsah came in with bread, Tamar rose and took the small basket from her nurse, nodding for her to take a place on a cushion near the door. Propriety must be maintained.

"Acsah has made bread, my lord." When he said nothing, Tamar broke the loaf and placed a portion before him. She poured a cup of goat's milk, took a small bunch of grapes from a platter, and cut into a pomegranate. She broke the fruit open so that the succulent red beads could be easily removed. "Is your father, Jacob, well?"

"As well as can be expected for a man mourning the loss of a favorite son," Judah said bitterly.

"One of your brothers has died?"

Judah raised his head from his hands and looked at her. "Years ago. Before you were even born."

"And still he grieves?" she said in wonder.

"He'll go to his grave grieving for that boy."

Never had Tamar seen such a look of torment. She pitied Judah and wished she knew some way to draw him from his sorrow. His expression softened slightly. The intensity of his perusal discomforted her, especially when his eyes cooled. "He marked your face!"

She covered her cheek quickly and turned her face away. "It's nothing." She never spoke of Er's abuse to anyone. Even when Acsah asked her questions, she refused to be disloyal to her husband. "Do you also grieve for your brother?"

"I grieve over the way he died."

Curious at his tone, she glanced at him again. "How did he die?"

Judah's face hardened. "He was torn apart by an animal. Nothing was found of him but his coat covered with blood." The words came as though he had said them over and over again and loathed repeating them. When she raised her brow, his expression was one of challenge. "You don't believe me?"

"Why should I not believe you?" She didn't want to anger him. "I would like to know more about my family."

"*Your* family?" His mouth curved ruefully.

Heat filled her cheeks. Did he mean to exclude her too? Anger stirred, along with hurt feelings. It was Judah who had brought her into this household, Judah who had chosen her for his son! Surely he would do right by her. "The family into which you brought me, my lord, a family I want to serve, if only I am allowed."

"If God is willing . . ." His mouth curved sadly. He took a piece of bread and began to eat.

"Will you tell me nothing?" she said weakly, her courage dwindling.

"What do you want to know?"

"Everything. Anything. Especially about your god. Where does he dwell? What is his name? How do you worship him? Is he unseen, as my father claims? How do you know he exists?"

Judah drew back. "I thought you wanted to know about my father and my brothers."

"I have heard that the god of your father destroyed the cities that were in the salt flat where the marsh now expands."

"That's true." He looked away. "The Angel of the Lord told Abraham He would destroy them unless ten righteous men could be found among those living there. Abraham saw with his own eyes the fire and brimstone that came down from heaven." Judah looked at her solemnly. "It doesn't matter if you can't see or hear Him. He doesn't live in temples like the gods of your father. He is . . ."

"Is . . . what?"

"Just . . . *is*. Don't pester me with questions. You're a Canaanite. Just go and pick an idol from Bathshua's cabinet and worship it!" His tone was derisive.

Her eyes pricked hot with tears. "You are the head of this household."

Color surged into Judah's face and his mouth tightened. Grimacing, he searched her face. He frowned slightly, then spoke softly. "The God of Jacob turns rock into springs of water. Or can crush a man's life with a thought." His eyes were bleak.

"Where does he dwell?"

"Anywhere He wants. Everywhere." Judah shrugged. "I can't explain what I don't understand." He frowned, his gaze distant. "Sometimes I don't want to know. . . ."

"How did your people come to know of him?"

"He spoke to Abraham, and He has spoken to my father."

"As you and I are speaking? Why would a god of such power lower himself to speak to a mere man?"

"I don't know. When Abraham first heard Him, He was . . . a voice. But the Lord comes anytime and in any way He wishes. He spoke to Abraham face-to-face. My father wrestled a blessing from Him. The Angel of the Lord touched my father's hip and crippled him forever. Sometimes He speaks in . . . dreams." The last seemed to trouble him deeply.

"Has he ever spoken to you?"

"No, and I hope He never does."

"Why?"

"I know what He would say." Judah sighed heavily and leaned back, tossing the bread onto the tray.

"Every god demands a sacrifice. What sacrifice does your god require?"

"Obedience." He waved his hand impatiently. "Don't ask me any more questions. Give me peace!"

Blushing, she murmured an apology. She was no better than Bathshua, battering him with her needs, her desires. Ashamed, Tamar withdrew. "Do you wish me to ask Bathshua to serve you?"

"I'd rather be stung by a scorpion. I want to be alone."

Acsah followed her from the room. "What did you say to upset him so?"

"I merely asked a few questions."

"What sort of questions?"

"Just questions, Acsah. Nothing that need concern you." Acsah would not comprehend her quest for understanding the God of Judah's fathers. Acsah worshiped the same gods Bathshua and her sons did, the same gods Tamar's mother and father and sisters and brothers worshiped. Why was she so different? Why did she hunger and thirst for something more?

"Everything you do concerns me," Acsah said, clearly annoyed. "I am your nurse, am I not?"

"I don't need one today." She couldn't tell Acsah that she wanted to know about the God of Judah. While everyone around her worshiped idols of stone, wood, or clay, she merely pretended. The gods of her father and mother had mouths but never spoke. They had eyes, but could they see? They had feet but never walked. Could they think or feel or breathe? And she had seen a truth about them: Those who worshiped them became like them, cold and hard. Like Bathshua. Like Er. Like Onan. Someday, Shelah would be the same.

There was nothing cold about Judah. She felt his brokenness. She saw his anguish. Why didn't the others who were supposed to love him? His wife! His sons! They didn't seem to care about anyone but themselves.

Judah was a Hebrew and strong; yet Tamar saw he was bitterly unhappy and tormented. He never seemed to have a moment's peace, even when left alone and in silence. Everything couldn't be blamed on a selfish, contentious wife and quarrelsome sons. There must be other reasons, deeper and more complex. If Bathshua knew what they were, she never spoke of them to anyone. She didn't even seem to care what her husband suffered. She merely complained that Judah brooded every time he returned from seeing Jacob.

Tamar frowned, wondering.

Perhaps Judah's despair had something to do with his father's grieving.

And the brother who had been lost.

✦ ✦ ✦

Judah wished he hadn't returned to his house so quickly. Far better had he returned to his flocks and seen to the animals Er too often neglected in his absence. His eldest had handed the full responsibility over to Onan after three short days! Er was a fool and useless as a shepherd. He had no love for the sheep that would one day belong to him. The boy stood by while wolves ripped open the belly of a defenseless ewe, then ran the predators off to become one himself. Er took pleasure in delivering the deathblow to a prized ram. Then he roasted and ate the meat!

Sometimes Judah looked at his boys and saw everything he'd worked to build going bad. He saw Simeon and Levi. He saw himself.

And he saw Joseph being led away in the shimmering heat of the desert sun.

Judah had thought he could run away. He thought he could shrug off the responsibility.

Sometimes he'd think back to the early days with Canaanite companions. His Adullamite friend Hirah had had all the answers. "Eat, my brother; drink; enjoy life to the fullest! Where passion burns, blow on the flames."

And Judah had burned. He'd craved corruption, hoping forgetfulness would come. Drink enough, and the mind clouds. Sleep with brazen temple prostitutes, and your senses melt away your conscience. After giving in to his

jealousy and anger against Joseph, why not give in to
every other emotion that pulled at him? Why not allow
instinct to reign? Why not give lust control? He'd wanted
desperately to become hard enough to feel no shame.
Maybe then the memory of his young brother would cease
to haunt him.

But nothing obliterated or softened the memory. It
haunted him still.

Often, when he was out alone, staring up at the heavens,
he wondered what had happened to Joseph. Were the boy's
bones bleached alongside the road to Egypt, or had he, by
some miracle, survived the journey? If so, was he now a
slave toiling under the desert sun, without hope or future?

No matter what Judah did, his life had the stench of
ashes. He couldn't escape the result of his actions. It was
too late to find and rescue his brother. Too late to save
him from a life worse than death. Too late to undo the sin *sinful*
that poisoned his own life. He'd committed a sin so hei- *man,*
nous, so unforgivable, he would go down to Sheol with it *overbearing*
blackening his soul. Every time he saw his father, shame *woman.*
filled him. Regret choked him. He couldn't look into
Jacob's eyes because he saw the unspoken question there:
*What really happened in Dothan? What did you and your
brothers do to my beloved son? Judah, when will you tell me
the truth?*

And Judah could feel his brothers' eyes upon him, waiting, breath held in fear that he would confess.

Even now, after all the years that had passed, the old
anger rose in him. The jealousy burned. He longed to cry
out and shake off the mantle of shame. *If you knew us so*

well, Father, why did you send the boy? Why did you give him into our hands when you knew we hated him so much? Were you that blind? And then the pain would return. Joseph hadn't been Jacob's favorite simply because he was the son of his father's favorite wife, Rachel. Joseph had deserved Jacob's love. The boy had always run to do his father's bidding, poured himself out to please him, while the rest always pleased themselves.

As much as Judah wanted to cast away the blame for getting rid of Joseph, it stuck like tar. Sin clung to him, soaked in, sank deep, until he felt his blood ran black with it. He was guilty, *and he knew it!*

And now Er's young wife was asking him about God. Judah didn't want to talk about God. He didn't want to think about Him.

Soon enough, he would face Him.

+ + +

Judah sent word to Onan and Shelah to bring the flocks home. Then he commanded Bathshua to prepare a feast.

"What for? It's not the new moon yet."

"I intend to discuss the future with my sons." He picked up his mantle and walked out into the night. He preferred the darkness and sounds of night creatures to the lamplight and carping sounds of his nagging wife.

Bathshua followed him outside. "They already know what the future holds! They've talked about it many times."

"They haven't talked with me!"

She put her hands on her hips. "What sort of trouble do you intend to bring upon my house now, Judah?"

He gritted his teeth. "Certain things need to be made clear."

"What things?" She was like a dog with a bone. She wouldn't let go.

"You'll know everything when they do."

"They're *my* sons. I know them better than you do! You could at least help me keep peace around here! Tell me what you plan to do. I will try to prepare them."

Judah glared back at her. "That's been the problem from the beginning, Bathshua. I've given you a free hand, and you've ruined *my* sons."

"*I've* ruined them! They're just like you: stubborn, foul tempered, constantly warring with one another! All they can think of is themselves!"

Judah strode away.

+   +   +

Tamar had known from the beginning that the feast would end in disaster. Bathshua had spent the entire day burning incense on her private altar and praying to her gods while Tamar, Acsah, and the servants saw to the preparations for the feast Judah ordered. Her mother-in-law was in bad temper, more fractious than usual, tense and looking for trouble. Tamar didn't intend to make matters worse by asking why Bathshua was so distressed over a father gathering his sons to talk about the future.

Er provided a fattened lamb. Tamar overheard one of the servants say he'd probably stolen it, but Bathshua asked no questions. She quickly ordered it slaughtered and spitted for roasting. Fresh bread was made and placed in baskets. Fruit and nuts mounded on trays. Bathshua commanded that all the jugs be filled with wine.

"Water and milk will make for a more amicable evening,"

Tamar said. Er was given to excess and would undoubtedly drink until he was drunk. Surely Bathshua knew that as well as she did.

Bathshua sneered. "Men prefer wine. So we'll give them wine, and plenty of it."

"But, Bathshua—"

"Mind your own business! This is my house, and I'll do as I please." She moved around the room, kicking cushions into place. "Judah commanded a feast, and a feast he'll get. Whatever happens will be on his head!" Her eyes glittered with tempestuous tears.

Judah's sons began feasting before Judah returned to the house. Tamar thought Judah's temper would erupt when he saw them, but he took his place calmly and ate without saying a word. His sons had already taken the best morsels for themselves. Er was already drunk and in the midst of telling how one of his friends had tripped a blind man walking along the road to Timnah.

"You should have seen him scrambling around like a snake on its belly, trying to find his stick." He laughed and tossed some grapes into his mouth. "'Over there,' I'd say, 'over there,' and the old fool would grovel in the dust. He never even came close to the stick. He's probably still trying to find the road." He threw back his head and laughed, his mother joining in.

Tamar tried not to show her disgust.

Er held out his cup. "More wine, Wife." He made her title sound like an insult. As she poured, he looked at the others. "Wait until I tell you how I got the goat."

Judah tossed his bread back into the basket. "You've said enough. Now I have something to say."

Er grinned. "That's why we're all here, Father. To hear whatever it is you have to say."

"It isn't settled in my mind who will be my heir."

The words were like a lightning strike in the room. There was sudden silence, crackling tension. Tamar looked at the members of the family. Bathshua sat pale and tense, her hands balled into fists. Er's face, already flushed from too much wine, turned dark red. Onan's eyes glowed. Shelah was the least affected, already asleep from too much wine.

"*I'm* your heir," Er said. "I'm the firstborn!"

Judah looked at him calmly, his eyes steady and cool. "It's my decision. If I want to give everything to my servant, I can."

"How can you even suggest such a thing?" Bathshua cried out.

Judah ignored her, his gaze still fixed upon his eldest son. "The sheep don't prosper in your care. Nor does your wife."

Tamar felt the heat flood her face and then drain away as her husband and mother-in-law turned their attention to her. Both spoke at once. Er called her a foul name, while Bathshua came to his swift defense. "She has no right to complain!" Bathshua said, glaring at her.

"Tamar hasn't uttered a word of complaint," Judah said coldly, "but anyone with half a brain and eyes in his head can see the treatment she receives at *your* son's hands."

"If you're wondering about the bruise on her face, Father,

she fell against the door a few days ago. Didn't you, Tamar? *Tell him!*"

"Perhaps you tripped her the same way you tripped that blind man along the road."

Er paled, but his eyes were like hot coals. "You're not going to take away what's mine."

"You still don't understand, Er, do you? Nothing belongs to you unless I say it does."

Tamar had never heard Judah speak so quietly or so coldly and with such authority. In this frame of mind, he was a man to be respected and feared. For the first time since she had entered his household, she admired him. She hoped he wouldn't weaken.

"Nothing will be taken from my hand unless I offer it," Judah said, his look encompassing Bathshua and her sons. "I gathered you here tonight to tell you that the one who proves himself the best shepherd will inherit my flocks."

"Is this a test?" Er was contemptuous. "Is that it?" He sneered. "Give the flocks to Onan now, if it pleases you, Father. Do you think it'll matter in the end? Onan is better with sheep, but I am better with a sword!"

"Do you see what you've done?" Bathshua cried out. "You've turned my sons against each other."

"After I'm gone, it's God who will decide what will happen."

"Yes," Er said, lifting his head as well as his cup. "Let the gods decide!" Wine sloshed over his hand as he proposed a toast. "In praise to the gods of Canaan! I vow to give my first daughter to the temple in Timnah and my first son to the fires of Molech!"

Tamar uttered a cry of despair at the same time Judah rose in anger. *"No!"*

She couldn't breathe. Would she conceive and bear children only to see them die in the flames of Topheth or perform intercourse on a public altar?

Er's pride burned white-hot. He rose as well and faced his father defiantly. "Do you think I care what you do? *My brothers will follow me,* Father. They will do as I do, or I will—" He stopped as though the breath had been drawn from him. His face changed; his eyes widened with fear. The cup dropped from his hand, splashing a red stain down the front of his fine tunic. He clutched at his chest.

Bathshua screamed. "Do something, Judah! *Help him!*"

Er tried to speak and couldn't. He clawed at his throat as though trying to pull hands away. Shelah, who had awakened at his mother's screaming, scrambled back, crying, while Onan watched Er drop to his knees. Judah reached out to his son, but Er pitched forward and fell facedown into the platter of roasted meat. He lay still.

"Er!" Bathshua said. "Oh, *Er!*"

Tamar was trembling violently, her heart galloping. She knew she should go to her husband's aid, but she was too afraid to move.

Bathshua pushed at Judah. "Leave my son alone. This is your fault!"

Judah shoved Bathshua back and went down on one knee. He put his hand against his son's neck. When he drew back, Tamar saw her own terror mirrored in his eyes. "He's dead."

49

"He can't be!" Bathshua said, pushing forward, falling to her knees beside Er. "You're wrong, Judah. He's drunk. He's just . . ."

When Bathshua managed to roll him over, she saw his face and screamed.

three

TAMAR wept with Judah's family during the formal mourning period. Judah was convinced God had struck down his firstborn son, and Bathshua, refusing to believe it, was inconsolable. Onan pretended to grieve, but Tamar saw him talking and laughing with some of the young Canaanite men who had called themselves Er's friends.

Tamar was ashamed of her own feelings. She wanted to mourn Er as a wife should, but she found herself weeping more in relief than sorrow, for she'd despised her husband. He'd held her captive in fear, and now she was free! Mingled with her grief was a deep fear of the God of Judah, who clearly possessed the power of life and death. She was more deeply afraid of this God than she had been of any man. When the Lord, the God of Abraham, Isaac, and Jacob, had struck down Judah's eldest and most rebellious son, this God had also delivered her from a life of misery. One moment Er was breathing vows to sacrifice his children and lead his brothers astray, and the next he was dead!

Her emotions were so confused, for the truth of her situation came to roost and feast upon her thoughts. She was not delivered at all, for now she was a widow. Her situation was no better than before. In fact, it was worse! She had no husband, no son, no standing in this household. She couldn't go home. Unless Judah did what custom demanded and gave her Onan as a husband, Tamar knew she would never bear sons or daughters at all. Her life would be useless. She would live without hope.

Only a son could deliver her!

The days passed slowly, and Judah said nothing. Tamar was patient. She hadn't expected him to speak of the matter during the mourning period. He would do what he must, for he was wise enough to know he couldn't leave things as they were and have his household prosper and grow. Judah's clan needed sons and daughters, or his household would diminish and die out.

Her failure to provide children made her a failure as a woman. Judah had chosen her to bear children for his household, and her position was unchanged. She was still the girl Judah had chosen. Judah must give her Onan as a husband. Onan must sleep with her and provide a son to inherit Er's portion. It was the way of both Canaanite and Hebrew. Brother must uphold brother.

Knowing this, Tamar didn't spend her time worrying about when Judah would make the decision. Instead, she spent her time wondering about the God of the Hebrews.

Her heart trembled when she considered the power He held. She was filled with questions but had no one to ask. Judah had made it clear he didn't want to talk about the God of his father.

So she rolled the questions over and over in her mind, seeking answers by herself and finding none. If God struck down Er for promising his children to the gods of Canaan, why hadn't He struck down Judah for allowing Bathshua to train up his sons in the worship of Baal? Or was the misery in Judah's life the curse laid upon him for some unknown act of rebellion? Judah had said once that the hand of God was against him. He was convinced; therefore, it must be true. Judah would know, wouldn't he? Fear filled Tamar at such thoughts, for if the hand of God was against Judah, what hope had any member of his family?

How do you soften the heart of a God who is angry with you? How do you placate Him when you don't know what He wants from you? What do you offer as sacrifice? What gift can you give? *Obedience,* Judah had said, but Tamar didn't know the rules to obey.

The fear of the Lord was upon her. Yet, even in her fear, Tamar felt strangely comforted. Er was no longer her master. Her fate was now in the hands of Judah. Not once during the year she'd been in this household had she ever seen her father-in-law offer sacrifices to the gods of Canaan. It was Bathshua who worshiped Baal and Asherah and a dozen others with fervent devotion. She was the one who poured out wine and oil, and cut herself. Judah kept his distance, and Bathshua never opened the cabinet where she kept her teraphim when Judah was within sight of it.

But Tamar had never seen Judah give offerings to his God either.

Did he do so when pasturing his sheep? Did he worship when he was with his father or his brothers? Her father-in-law never said anything one way or the other, and Tamar dared not inquire of Bathshua.

If the God of Judah allowed, she would bear children by Onan, and she would fulfill the hope Judah had to build up his household. Er was dead. She would take comfort in knowing her children would never be placed in the arms of Molech and rolled into the fires of Topheth, nor would they be trained up to perform lewd acts with a priest on a public altar dedicated to Astarte. They would grow up in the ways of Judah's father and not in the ways of her own. They would bow down to Judah's God and not bend to those of Bathshua.

Her heart cried out for this to be true, though nothing was certain. A year in Judah's household had taught Tamar that Bathshua had the upper hand. On the one occasion Judah had exerted his authority, his eldest son had rebelled and died.

She couldn't go to Judah and talk of these things. It was too soon, too painful. When Judah was ready, he would send for her. What else could he do? She was to be the childbearer.

+ + +

Judah pondered the future of his family. He knew what he had to do but still waited seventy days before summoning Tamar. When she stood before him in her black *tsaiph,* slender and dignified, her head up, he realized she had changed. Her face no longer bore the marks of ill treatment. Her skin was smooth and healthy. Yet it was more than that. Poised and calm, she looked at him. She was no longer the trembling child-bride he had brought home to Er.

Judah knew Tamar had never loved Er. She had submitted to Er, showing his son the respect due a husband. Though he knew she'd been beaten, Judah had never seen her cower like a dog. She had accepted her fate and worked hard to become part of his family. She had submitted to every command. She would accept his decision now and abide by it.

"I'm giving Onan to you as your husband so that you can bear a son for Er."

"My lord," she said and bowed down to him.

Judah wanted to say something, anything that might give the poor girl comfort and hope. But what could he say that wouldn't demean Er? No matter how bent upon evil his eldest son had been, Er was still the first fruit of Judah's loins, the first show of his strength as a man. He couldn't speak against Er without speaking against himself.

A blessing would ease his conscience. "May you be fruitful and multiply my house, Tamar." She would not suffer with Onan. As far as Judah knew, his second son took no pleasure in tormenting the helpless.

When Tamar rose to her feet, she lifted her head and looked at him. He was discomfited by the warmth in her eyes. He nodded. "You may go."

She turned away and then turned back again. "May I speak with you, my lord?" Something plagued her deeply.

He raised his brows.

"Since I am to bear children for your household, will you instruct me in the ways of your God?"

He stiffened. "When the time comes, I will speak to Onan about it."

"Surely the time is long past."

He clenched his fists. "Do you dare reprimand me?"

"No, my lord," she said in confusion. She paled. "I beg your pardon. I only meant . . ."

He saw the tears well in her eyes but ignored her appeal. "Leave me." Closing his eyes, he jerked his head in command. He heard her quick retreating footsteps.

Why did Tamar always have to ask about God? What could he tell her? God had struck Er for his cruel arrogance and taken vengeance upon Judah as well. An eye for an eye, a life for a life. Er for Joseph.

Judah raked his fingers through his hair, then held his head. Perhaps now the past could be laid to rest.

"This is what he requires: to do what is right, to love mercy, and to walk humbly with your God." His father's words came to him as though Jacob had leaned close and whispered them.

Agitated, Judah rose and left the house.

+   +   +

Tamar returned to her quarters and told Acsah what had been said. Onan was to sleep with her and give her children for Er.

"Judah spoke with me eight days ago," Acsah said. "He has been counting the days."

Tamar blushed.

Acsah smiled at her. "Onan is a better man than Er. He won't beat you."

Tamar lowered her eyes. Onan was as handsome as Er. He could speak as smoothly. He might also have fists like hammers. She breathed in slowly. She couldn't allow herself to dwell on fear. Fear might prevent conception.

Despite her resolve, her stomach quivered with misgivings. She had no reason to expect tender treatment from Onan. Why should she? He kept company with the same young men Er did.

Acsah took her by the shoulders. "Be joyful, Tamar. Judah's taken your side against Bathshua."

Tamar shrugged her hands away. "Don't be foolish, Acsah. There are no sides to this matter. It is but a thing of necessity."

"A thing of necessity? How you talk! Your mother-in-law has burned Judah's ear for weeks regarding you. She didn't want Onan in the same room with you, let alone the same bed."

"Can you blame her? I would grieve as much if I'd lost a son."

"Or a loving husband." She lowered her voice to a conspiratorial whisper. "We're all well rid of Er."

Tamar turned away, unwilling to agree.

Acsah sighed. "You must be careful, Tamar. Bathshua seeks someone to blame."

Tamar sat on a cushion. "Then she must look to the God of Judah."

"She suspects *you*. She claims you cast a spell."

Tamar glanced up sharply. "What power have I to help or hinder anyone in this household? I am nothing! What did I have to gain by my husband's death? Am I better off now with my husband dead?" She shook her head and looked away. "No one will believe Bathshua. Everyone heard Er reject the God of his father, and everyone saw how he died."

Acsah hunkered down before her. "Do you think that matters?" She took Tamar's hands and held them tightly. "Much of the blame for Er's character can be laid at his mother's feet, but do you think she will ever accept it?"

Tamar pulled her hands from Acsah's and covered her face. "I did nothing to harm Er!" She drew a ragged breath, tears welling despite her efforts to quell them. "What sort of household is this that everyone seeks to destroy each other?"

Acsah pressed her fingertips against Tamar's lips. "I know you did nothing to harm Er. So does Judah. Not once did you ever speak against Er. Everyone knew he beat you, and they all looked the other way."

"Then how can you say . . . ?"

"You're too young to understand the ways of people like Bathshua. She's jealous. She's afraid of losing her position. So she lies. A lie told often enough will eventually be accepted as truth."

"I can only be what I am, Acsah!" Tears ran down her cheeks. "I can only live the best way I know how."

Acsah cupped her cheek. "Be at peace, my sweet one. You have prevailed. Judah has given Onan to you. It shows he believes the god of his father took his son's life despite Bathshua's claims that you had a part in it. But be warned: She is as cunning as a serpent. She will be silent now that Judah has made his decision. For a while she will do nothing. But never forget: She is your enemy."

"As she always has been, Acsah."

"More now than ever, but Judah will protect you."

With a sad laugh, Tamar shook her head. "Judah stands neither to the right nor to the left of me. He stands alone, just as he always has. All he's done is take the necessary steps to preserve his family." She turned away, not wanting Acsah to see her hurt and disappointment. Judah had refused to instruct her in the ways of his God, even though this God clearly had the power of life and death. "I am more burdened now than I was the day I came here, Acsah. I want this household to prosper. I want to fulfill my duty."

"You will."

"If I have children."

"When, not if." Acsah smiled. "Onan will give you a child. I've no doubt of that."

Tamar didn't share her confidence. Onan was, after all, Er's brother.

✦   ✦   ✦

Acsah was pleased that Judah had finally settled the matter. Her heart ached as she witnessed the indifference in this household. No one in this household deserved Tamar. She was lovely and sweet, hardworking, loyal. Acsah's heart sometimes swelled with pride as she watched the way the girl conducted herself with dignity, especially when faced with Bathshua's slights, insults, and outbursts. There were times when Acsah had had to bite her tongue so she would not speak her mind and cause Tamar more trouble.

Judah had delayed long enough in giving Onan to Tamar. Acsah had begun to fear that Bathshua had succeeded in poisoning him against Tamar. She loved Tamar as dearly as she would have loved any child of her own womb, and it angered her to watch how she was treated.

Acsah had rejoiced when Judah sought her out and asked about Tamar's health. He'd been uncomfortable. She'd understood what he was really asking and spared him further embarrassment. "The best time for conception would be in ten days."

"Ten days. You're certain?"

"Yes, my lord." Acsah hadn't neglected her duty toward Tamar or Judah's household. The girl had no secrets from her. It was Acsah's duty to watch over Tamar's health. She knew the days of her cycle. She counted them from the full moon so that she would know precisely which days offered greatest fertility.

Even though the matter of Onan was settled, Acsah was worried about Tamar's mood. Tamar was pensive and secretive. Before, she had always shared her thoughts and feelings. Acsah knew it was because the girl was becoming a woman, but it hurt to be excluded even in these small ways. She adored the girl and sought only the best for her. How could she lift her spirits when she didn't know what Tamar was thinking? She pressed, but Tamar resisted. She wouldn't say what was wrong. Acsah could only assume it was fear at the prospects of physical intimacy with Onan. And she could easily understand that, considering the heartless treatment her dear girl had suffered at Er's hands. Acsah had been afraid for her and distressed about what to do without causing more trouble for her. A bruise now and then was common enough, but harder blows could cause internal injuries and permanent damage. And then what would become of Tamar?

But Er was dead now. Secretly, Acsah rejoiced. The wretched boy had only gotten what he deserved. He would never lay another hand upon Tamar, and Acsah was thankful to whatever god had struck him down. Countless times she had wished *she* had the power to do it. She had had to plug her ears to keep from going mad when she heard Tamar's muted cries of pain behind closed doors.

Tamar need not fear Onan. Judah's second son was different from the first. Onan was shrewd and ambitious. He tended his father's flocks as though they were already his own. Acsah suspected Onan coveted more than his brother's inheritance. He'd coveted his brother's wife as well. Acsah had noticed the way the boy looked at Tamar. Perhaps the boy's lust would turn to love, and Tamar's life would be easier.

Most assuredly, Onan would be eager to fulfill his duty to her. The first son Tamar bore would be for Er, but others would follow. They would belong to Onan. Acsah could hardly wait for the day to come when she would help Tamar bring a child into the world. Oh, to see her lovely smile bloom again, to hear her laugh, to see her eyes shine with happiness! Tears sprang to Acsah's eyes just thinking about it.

Taking her broom and basket, Acsah entered the room where Tamar and Onan would lie together. She set the basket by the door and worked vigorously. She chanted as she did so, exorcising the divine assembly from the room. Some spirits liked to hinder desire and prevent conception. They must be swept out and prevented from coming back. It was Acsah's duty to see to this. She must protect the young couple and open the way to unfettered lovemaking.

Acsah took great care in her work. She made sure every inch of the walls, ceiling, and floor were swept. Then she

mixed mortar and caulked the holes in the stone wall so that
evil spirits couldn't enter through them. She brought in
rush mats and laid them out neatly over the earthen floor.
She filled small lamps with scented oil and placed trays of
incense in each of the four corners of the room. The air of
the bedchamber would be permeated with a sweet musky
fragrance that would stir the senses and stimulate desire.
She took a mandrake from her basket and shaved off slivers
of the precious root into a cup beside a jug of wine.
Mandrake would increase Tamar's fertility. Last, she took
out a woven cloth and spread it over the mat where the
couple would lie together.

Standing in the doorway, Acsah scrutinized every aspect
of the room. She must make certain everything was in
place, nothing forgotten. Voices and music came from the
main room. The wedding feast had begun. Soon she would
lead the couple to this chamber.

As a last precaution, Acsah entered the room again and
took fine ground flour from a pouch at her waist. She cast it
over the floor from the edge of the walls to the doorway.
With every sweep of her arm, she chanted incantations to
drive spirits from the room. She wasn't satisfied until a thin
layer of flour covered everything. If any spirits returned,
she would see footprints in the pale dust and be warned of
their presence.

Acsah closed the door firmly. She filled in the crack
around the door until the room was sealed.

Finally, satisfied, she sat and rested. She would give Tamar
an hour more to celebrate. Perhaps a cup or two of wine
would make Tamar relax and enjoy herself. Smiling, Acsah

murmured prayers to her gods. Soon she would lead the young couple to the bedchamber. She would make sure no spirits had entered, and then she would close the door behind Onan and Tamar and remain on guard against the spirits who might try to hinder conception. She would sit against the closed door and she would play her small drum, and she would sing a song to drive demons away and make young hearts beat with passion. If the jealous spirits could be kept from the house long enough, Tamar would conceive. And then, finally, this girl Acsah loved and served would be given the respect she was due as a childbearer.

✦ ✦ ✦

Tamar soon learned that Onan was different from Er: His evil was more cunning.

Even while Tamar's head swam with wine and her senses with the scents of sweet herbs and sound of Acsah's drum, she knew the exact moment Er's brother denied her the chance of a child. She cried out, but he covered her mouth with his own, silencing her protest. She struggled fiercely and wrenched free, clambering away from him.

"You've dishonored me!" She snatched her garment and covered herself. "And betrayed your own brother!"

Onan sat up, breathing heavily. "I promise, I'll treat you better than Er ever did."

"And this is better?"

"I'll treat you with kindness and . . ."

"Kindness?" Er had abused her. Now Onan was using her. "We're together for one purpose: to conceive a son for Er."

Onan stretched out on his side. "What's wrong with enjoying ourselves?"

Tamar glared at him without response.

Onan's eyes narrowed. "Stop looking at me like I'm an insect you found under a rock."

"You must fulfill your duty to my dead husband, your brother."

"I *must?*" Onan's face darkened. "Who are you to tell me I must?"

"You know who I am and what my position is in this house. Will you do what is right or not?"

"I promise to take care of you. You'll always have a roof over your head and food to eat. I'll give you all you require."

Her face went hot. Did he really think she would allow him to treat her like a prostitute? She could hardly stand to look at him. "There's only one thing I require of you, Onan, and you've spilled that on the ground!" She flung his discarded tunic at him.

Slipping into it, Onan blushed, but his eyes remained calculating. "Er said you were stubborn. You could try to understand my situation."

She wasn't a fool. She knew exactly what he was after. She had known Onan was covetous, but she'd never expected this abominable injustice. "You want Er's double portion as well as your own!" Onan was filled with avarice.

"Why shouldn't I have it all? I've worked for it!"

"You have your portion. You have no right to Er's. It belongs to his son."

He smirked. "What son?"

Her eyes pricked with angry tears. "You will *not* have your way in this, Onan. I am not a harlot to be used."

"Be reasonable, Tamar. Did Er ever care for the flocks as I have? Have I hit you or called you names? Did he ever show kindness toward you? Even once? All my brother ever did was cause you grief!"

"It doesn't matter how he treated me or anyone else! He is your father's eldest son. Er was firstborn. You must fulfill your duty to your brother, or his line will die! Do you think Judah won't grieve over what you've done tonight?"

"Don't tell him."

"I won't join you in this sin. What future have I if you have your way?"

"The future I give you."

"And I should trust a man who denies his brother an heir?"

Onan stood, annoyed. "Er's name should be wiped out! He deserved to die! We're all better off without him!"

Tamar was shocked by his hatred. "You mustn't deny me my rights, Onan. If you do, you cheat your father's entire household."

Jaw tight, Onan made a sound of disdain. "You don't know what I suffered at my brother's hands. Every time my mother looked the other way, Er was using his fists on me. I'm glad he's dead. If you want to know the truth, I rejoiced when Er choked to death. It gave me pleasure to watch him die. I wanted to laugh and dance!" He smiled down at her mockingly. "As I'm sure you did."

"Don't include me in your wickedness. Er's portion doesn't belong to you. It belongs to the son he might have had, the son you *must* give me."

Onan lay down again and propped himself up on one elbow. "And if I won't?"

"You can't really mean to deny me, Onan. Would you have Er's name go down into the dust with him?" It was as though he sought to murder his own brother.

"That's where his name belongs."

What Onan was doing was worse than murder! He was denying existence to all of Er's descendants down through the ages. If he had his way, she would never bear children. What would become of her then?

"Please, Onan. You mustn't do this. Give thought to what you do!"

"I have thought about it. It's *my* name I care about, not his."

"What sort of man are you that you would destroy the household of your own brother?"

"What brother? What household?" He laughed softly. He took the edge of her wrap and rubbed it between his fingers. "I'm a man who intends to hold on to what belongs to him." He grinned. "I can make you happy. Would you like me to show you how?"

Tamar yanked her wrap from him and withdrew even farther. She wanted to scream at Acsah to stop beating the drum and singing. This night was a mockery!

Onan's expression cooled. "Be satisfied with what I'm offering you."

His avarice sickened her. "I won't keep silent."

"What can you do?" He mocked her just as Er had done.

"I can speak to Judah."

Onan laughed. "Go ahead. Father won't do anything. He never does anything. Besides, it will be your word against mine, and who will believe you, Tamar? My mother hates you with every breath she takes. Moreover, she's convinced you cast a spell upon my brother and caused his death." His smile derided her. "All I have to say is I gave my all to fulfill my duty, but the gods have closed your womb."

She blinked back tears. "I will tell your father the truth, and may the God of Judah judge between you and me!" She rose, intending to leave the room.

Onan lunged for her. She tried to dodge him, but he grasped her ankle. When she tried to kick free, he swept her feet out from under her. She came down hard, and he pinned her against the rush mats scattered on the earthen floor Acsah had taken such care in sweeping.

"Be satisfied with what you have, girl, for you will have no more of me than I intend to give! And when my father dies, you won't even have that much unless you make an effort to please me!"

Tamar drew in a sobbing breath and turned her face away. Onan eased his grip on her. "Shhhh . . ." He caressed her cheek and kissed her throat. "There now, my sweet little bride. Don't cry." His touch repulsed her. "Everyone's glad Er's dead and gone. You should be too." He cupped her face and made her look at him. "I still want you, Tamar. I've wanted you since the day you came here. And now you're mine." When he tried to kiss her, she jerked her face away. Gritting her teeth, Tamar shut her eyes tightly and didn't move.

"Make up your mind to enjoy things as they are. They won't change."

"I'd rather be dead."

Onan cursed. "Don't tempt me." The rush mats rustled softly as he moved away from her. "Have it your own way.

Have *nothing.*" He fell asleep within minutes, his conscience not the least disturbed.

Tamar slept in the corner, her hands over her head, while Acsah went on singing love songs outside the door.

✦   ✦   ✦

Tamar spent the night gathering her nerve. She was resolved to fight the injustice done her. It was within her rights, and she must gather the courage to do so. Surely Judah would defend her. Without children, his family would dwindle and die out. The wind would blow away the name of Judah as though it were dust. She must take courage. She must be strong. She would have to speak up for herself because the sons in this wretched household cared only about themselves!

She went to Judah before Onan was even awake. She told her father-in-law exactly what his son had done. She presented the cloth Acsah had placed upon the rush mat to prove her statement. Judah's face turned dark red.

"You've had only one night with Onan! He'll come to his senses. Give him time."

Time? Was that all Judah could say? He should be furious that his son had intended to deceive him. Onan was sinning against the entire household! His actions were clear, his motivation pure greed, and his crime equal to murder. How could Judah overlook this sin against his family? No matter how many times Er had abused her, she couldn't allow her dead husband to be so dishonored. Did she have to scream from the rooftop to make him call Onan to account?

"I will not allow Onan to touch me under these circumstances. I cannot!"

Judah's eyes flashed. "Who are you to tell me what will or will not go on in *my* household?"

"How can I allow this? I'm the wife of your firstborn son! Would you see Er's name die because Onan refused to do his duty?"

"Be silent, girl!"

Anger filled her. "I am a woman, Judah, and shouting at me will not drown out the truth of this humiliation!" She knew Judah didn't want to be pressed by anyone, but it was her right, indeed, her *obligation* to bear children. "Why do you thwart me? It's in all our interests that sons be born!" What would become of Judah's tribe if things were allowed to continue in such an immoral manner as this? "Land cannot be worked without children. Flocks cannot be tended without children."

"I don't need you to tell me that!"

Judah roared like a wounded lion, but Tamar refused to back down. Judah was not like Er. He wouldn't use his fists upon a woman. And she could take hot wind any day. "It is my right to have children!"

Judah turned his face away, the muscle working in his jaw. "Very well," he said grudgingly. "I'll speak to Onan when I get around to it. In the meantime, let things be as they are." He raised his hand when she started to protest. "Let me finish! Given time, my son may come to love you. Have you thought of that? You might work toward that end instead of causing him trouble. Do whatever you can to make him love you. If Onan loves you, he'll do right by you of his own accord, without my saying a word."

Her cheeks burned. Just as Onan had said, Judah would

do nothing. He would go off to tend his sheep and leave it in her hands to woo righteousness from Onan!

"Do you know so little of your own sons, Judah?" Er had been incapable of love, and Onan was eaten up with jealousy and avarice, his only ambition to grasp everything he could now that his older brother was dead and couldn't protect himself. Judah might as well have said it straight out: It was up to her to protect her husband's birthright and portion. It was up to her to find a way to have a child.

"I know my sons," Judah said grimly, glaring at her.

She fought her tears, for she knew Judah would have no respect for her if she shed them. "Why do you refuse to confront the sin that goes on before your eyes? You never called Er to account, and now you look the other way while Onan refuses—"

"Don't tell me how to run my life or my family!"

"I would never assume to usurp Bathshua's place!"

Judah's eyes widened in surprise, and then his face paled in rage. "You've said enough." He spoke with deadly calm.

Tamar saw his anger and didn't care. If he wanted to hit her, let him. She'd been hit before, and in this household she had no doubt she would be hit again. She would not face this lion like one of his sheep!

"When you gave the bride-price to my father, a covenant was made between you." It was all she could do to speak in quiet reason and not scream out her frustration. "I became the wife of your son Er, and as your son's wife, I became *your daughter*. Will you allow me to be treated like a harlot? Surely a man who defended his sister against the prince of Shechem—"

"Those circumstances were entirely different!" he interrupted, his face white.

Tamar realized she had torn open an old wound and tried to make amends. "I'm part of your family, Judah." Clearly, he didn't embrace her as a daughter, but he still owed her consideration. He couldn't allow her rights to be trodden beneath Onan's feet.

"Be patient, Tamar. I've lost Er. I don't want to battle Onan." He groaned in frustration. "There must be some other way!"

There was, but she loathed mentioning it. He must know as well as she did the only other alternative open to them. She swallowed hard, her cheeks going hot. "If you prefer, you can follow Canaanite custom and perform the duty yourself."

His head came up. Clearly, he thought her suggestion as repugnant as she did. "I'm Hebrew, not Canaanite."

"I meant no offense."

"If you were a woman fully grown, you could make Onan forget himself instead of dumping your problem in my lap!"

Her eyes welled with hurt tears. She was woman enough to conceive. That's all that was required of her. Or had he forgotten? Did she have to become wily and devious in order to fulfill her duty to *his* dead son? Did Judah expect her to behave like a harlot and take from Onan what he should freely give? Perhaps Judah expected her to run to her sister in Timnah and ask for instructions in the erotic arts! Perhaps she should adorn herself in veils and bells so Onan would be so overcome by lust that he would forget his greed and unwittingly fulfill his obligation!

Tamar trembled in anger.

Once again, Judah would turn away from his responsibilities. He wanted her to plot and scheme and entice Onan into doing what was right to save himself trouble.

"I will not play the harlot."

"Why not?" He gave a cynical laugh. "Women have done it for years."

"When will you do what is right?"

"Get out!"

Tamar fled the house in tears. Acsah followed. "What's happened, Tamar? What were you and Judah shouting about?"

Tamar took up her hoe and began beating the ground with it. Tears coursed down her cheeks, and she dashed them away and went on working.

"Tell me, Tamar. Did Onan mistreat you? Is he like Er after all?"

"Leave me alone, Acsah. Just let me work in peace." She would not pile further humiliation upon herself by sharing her shame and Judah's cowardice.

+ + +

Once again the conjugal room was prepared, for there were still six days remaining in the wedding week. Onan was in even higher spirits, sure that he had won his way. He held his head up like a triumphant warrior and took Tamar's hand as Acsah led them once again to the bedchamber. Tamar went willingly, hoping he would repent and fulfill his duty.

He did not.

While he slept, Tamar sat weeping in the farthest corner

of the room, her head covered with her black *tsaiph*. She was bereft, overcome with shame and humiliation. Onan was destroying her hope for an honorable future. If he had his way, she would never bear children for Judah's household. She might as well be dead!

It wasn't until the sun rose that Tamar found death *had* come.

And taken Onan.

four

THE household was in an uproar, and Tamar was in the middle. Those who hadn't believed Bathshua's stories about Tamar being somehow responsible for Er's death were now convinced she was responsible for Onan's. Even Tamar began to wonder if she was somehow to blame. Two husbands dead in a year's time? What ill fortune! How could this be? Her emotions were in tatters. Both Er and Onan had been wicked, but there were many wicked men who were walking and talking and carrying on as usual. Why had her husbands been singled out?

Tamar's throat closed hot; her eyes burned. She was innocent. She'd had nothing to do with these strange deaths, but rumors were rampant. Gossip ripped the household into factions, and Bathshua gossiped most of all. How could her mother-in-law call her a witch? She had never cast a spell or uttered an incantation. She wanted to defend herself, but every time she started to speak, she would see the look on others' faces and know it was no use. They already believed the lies and were afraid.

Tamar was afraid too. From the day she had entered this household, she'd been treated like a despised slave. Everyone knew Er had abused her, and yet no one had uttered a word of compassion or lifted a finger to help her. And now, even though Onan had used her for his selfish pleasure and had denied her right to mother an heir who would claim Er's portion, everyone believed she had wished him dead. It wasn't true! She had come into this household hoping to be a good wife and to bear children. It was the God of Judah's father who had struck these young men down. Hadn't Judah said as much himself the day Er died?

But Judah didn't say that anymore.

Judah didn't say *anything!* He brooded and guzzled wine to forget his troubles while Bathshua filled his ears with lies. Tamar knew it must be easier for her father-in-law to think she was at fault than believe his God was destroying his family. Who would be next? Shelah? Bathshua?

When Judah looked at her, she saw his anger, his suspicion. He sought someone to blame for his wretchedness. And everyone in the household pointed to her. That made it easier for Judah to cast blame as well.

Bathshua's hatred permeated the house. Tamar couldn't get away from it. Even when she was working outside, Tamar sensed Bathshua's malice. "I want her out of this house and away from my family!"

Didn't Bathshua understand that by stoking the fires that already burned, she was destroying her household? Why not plead with the God of Judah for mercy? Why not inquire of Jacob what must be done to turn the winds in their favor? Why did Judah sit and brood in silence and let his family fall apart around him? *Guilt, sin, Crap?*

Acsah urged Tamar repeatedly, "Try to speak with him, Tamar."

"I cannot. I won't respond to Bathshua's lies, even to defend myself."

"Everyone is against you!"

"If the God of Judah took Er and Onan, what can I do to make things right? It's up to Judah. He's the head of this house."

"Bathshua is the head."

"Judah has allowed it! Whatever happens to me is in his hands. All I can do is wait and see what he will do." Despite what people thought or said about her, custom still required Shelah to give her children. But would Judah follow through now that his second son was dead? Would he entrust Shelah to her with two sons already in the grave?

Tamar wept in secret at the cruel things said about her, but she maintained her composure in the presence of others. Even if she were to grovel and cower and plead before Bathshua, it wouldn't change the woman's blackened heart. Tamar strove to maintain her dignity before her enemies.

The mourning period passed, and the weeks wore on.

Tamar waited. Sooner or later her father-in-law would have to make a decision.

✦   ✦   ✦

Judah allowed seventy-five days to pass before he summoned Tamar. He had done nothing but think about the girl over the past weeks. She had a right to Shelah and children, but he was afraid his last son would die if he married her. Bathshua insisted Tamar was evil and casting spells, but why would the girl do such things? She needed sons to provide for her. She needed a husband to give her those sons. Why kill her best chances for a secure future? As a childless widow, she had no hope.

Bathshua remained bitter and adamant. "Don't give her my last son! I'll hate you for the rest of my life if you do! She mustn't have Shelah!" When Bathshua wasn't railing and threatening, she was seeking the counsel of her teraphim. The house was stifling with the cloying scent of incense. Every other day some medium was coming to the door, claiming to have messages from the dead.

"Get rid of Tamar." Bathshua was rabid. "Get that evil girl out of my house!"

Judah had never seen Tamar cast a spell or utter a single incantation, but that didn't mean she hadn't. She might not be as open as his wife, who had never made a secret of her passion for Canaanite deities.

Judah knew God had taken Er and that He had taken Onan as well. Perhaps, if he had done as Tamar asked and confronted Onan for his sin . . . Judah didn't think long on that possibility. God may have struck down his sons, but the girl was a bad omen. She'd been nothing but trouble since he brought her into his house. If he got rid of her, perhaps he would have some peace.

Shelah was the only son Judah had left. Bathshua was right. The boy must be protected. Tamar was the one constant in the midst of the disasters that had befallen his household. Judah couldn't risk Shelah's life by giving him to her. Besides, Shelah was afraid of Tamar. Bathshua had convinced the boy he would die if he lay with Tamar.

"When will you do what is right, Judah?"

Tamar's words pricked his conscience, but he hardened his heart against them. He was only protecting his family. Why should he give his last son to this dangerous girl? Why take any risk? Why drive a bigger wedge between himself and his wife? Why cause himself more grief?

Besides, Tamar was probably barren anyway. In all the months she'd been with Er, she hadn't conceived. She hadn't been desirable enough to sway Onan. Why should he waste Shelah on this wretched little witch? Shelah was his last surviving son, his only heir, his last hope. He wouldn't do it!

Judah sent for his son. "Go to Hirah and remain in Adullam until I send for you."

Relieved of his duty, Shelah praised his father's decision and obeyed with alacrity. Judah felt a twinge of shame, but it quickly disappeared. He'd protect his son—even at the cost of his own honor.

+   +   +

Tamar knew something more had gone wrong when Acsah came out to her and worked in disheartened silence. "What is it, Acsah? What's happened?"

"Judah sent Shelah away this morning."

Tamar's heart sank. "He must have sent him to see about the flocks."

"The flocks are not anywhere near Adullam, Tamar. That's where Shelah has gone."

Tamar looked at the ground she was working. "There's nothing I can do but wait, Acsah. And hope."

"Indeed, there is nothing you can do." Acsah wept.

When Judah sent for her, Tamar went eagerly, hoping he would have some explanation. However, the moment she saw her father-in-law, she knew Acsah was right. Shelah was gone, and there was nothing to be done about it.

"I've made a difficult decision," Judah said slowly, unable to look her in the eyes. "Shelah is too young to take on the responsibilities of a husband."

Shelah was two years older than she was, but Tamar didn't quibble. Judah was making excuses. They both knew it. Arguing with him now would only set his heart against her. Let Bathshua browbeat him with lies. The truth would become clear in time. She would be obedient. She would be patient. She would behave with dignity, even if he behaved with cowardice. Time was her ally. Time and necessity. Judah needed her. Er needed a son to carry on the family line. If Judah failed to grant Tamar the right to bear that son, he would be a man who had forsaken all honor. Could such a man ever be trusted?

"When Shelah is older, I will send for you."

Tamar blinked, confused. "Send for me?" What did he mean? She searched his face and saw his eyes grow hard.

"Bathshua is having your things packed as we speak. She will have one of the servants take you and your nurse back to your father's house."

"My father's house? But, my lord, this is—"

"Don't argue!" Judah wouldn't even allow her to open her mouth in her own defense. "This is best. You will remain in your father's house as a widow until I call for you."

"Best?" She was cold with shock. "Am I to be cast out for the sins done against *me?*"

"You're not being expelled. You're going home."

"This is my home. As cold and inhospitable as it's always been!"

"Say nothing more against my family. It's for their sakes I make this decision. Your presence has turned my household into a battlefield."

"You are *unjust!"* She began to cry, shaming herself completely.

He looked away. "Resorting to tears won't change my mind," he said coldly.

Anger spurred her. "Do you think my father will welcome me with open arms?" She struggled for control over her unraveling emotions. "A widow twice over? Childless? Rejected and cast out?"

Judah was implacable. "Tell him I want you to remain a widow in his house until Shelah has grown up. When that day comes, I will send for you."

Tamar lifted her head and stared into his eyes. "Will you?"

"I said I would."

She refused to look away. Let him see the faith she had in him now that he had forsaken her.

Judah's face reddened and his eyes shifted. "You don't believe me?"

She gave him no answer, though she wondered. When had she ever seen Judah do what was right?

"I promise you!" he said quickly. "There! Now will you go without more distress?"

Content with that, Tamar did as he commanded.

Bathshua stood just outside the door, triumphant and pitiless. "Your nurse is waiting for you outside." Fighting tears, Tamar stepped past her, but Bathshua wasn't satisfied. She followed Tamar to the door and stood watching. "We're well rid of you!"

Tamar didn't look back. Nor did she look at Acsah, afraid that if she did so, she'd burst into tears and give Bathshua even more satisfaction. "Judah is sending us back to my father."

Acsah's eyes flashed. "I shall lay a curse upon Bathshua and her household." She stepped forward, but Tamar grasped her arm, yanking her back.

"You will not! This is my home, my family. No matter what Judah thinks, this is where I belong."

Acsah's eyes filled with angry tears. "They do not deserve you," she said under her breath.

"Judah chose me, Acsah. I will live in hope of being worthy of his choice. If you must speak, say prayers on his family's behalf."

No servant was given to accompany or protect them. They were given two small barley loaves and a skin of water to share.

When Tamar was well out of sight of the house, she fell to her knees and sobbed. Filling her hands with dust, she covered her head. Unable to console her, Acsah wept as well.

It was only eight miles to Zimran's house. The hot sun

was heavy upon them, but not as heavy as their hearts. It was dusk before Tamar arrived at her father's door. He was not pleased to see her.

+   +   +

Zimran ordered everyone out. Tamar's mother, Acsah, her sisters and brothers all hastened to obey. She wished she could flee her father's wrath as well. She had no choice but to stand silent as he unleashed his fury upon her. Perhaps, in the end, he would show mercy.

"I gave you to Judah's son so that you would bear children for him and keep peace between us! You have failed me! You have failed us all!"

She must keep her wits about her, or she was lost. "Judah gave me his word that he would send for me when Shelah is old enough to fulfill his duty to me."

Zimran turned a scornful eye upon her. "And you believed that Hebrew? You fool! Shelah is only a few years younger than Er. Three or four at the most! And now Judah says Shelah isn't old enough yet to father children? *Ha!* If he's too young, why take him to the sheepshearing? You should have insisted upon your rights!"

She stumbled under the blow of his hand, falling to her knees. "I did all I could, Father."

"Not enough!" Zimran paced, his face red, his hands balled. "You should have remained in his house rather than come back here. What good are you to me? You bring shame upon my house!"

Tamar pressed a hand over her throbbing cheek. Her heart pounded with fear. She must not give in to it. She must *think*. "Judah promised, Father. He *promised.*"

"So what? What good are vows with a Hebrew? The Hebrews made an agreement with Shechem, didn't they? Look what happened to them!" He stood over her. "You're no longer my responsibility! If Judah doesn't want you in his house, why should I want you in mine? You'll bring us all ill fortune!"

She must survive. "If you're willing to risk it, Father, ignore Judah's wishes. Cast me out!"

"Judah's wishes? What wishes?"

"To build his household." Was her father still afraid of Judah? She could only hope so. "Will Bathshua bear more sons for Judah, Father? She's dry as dust and cold as stone. Can Judah give Shelah to another woman before he's fulfilled his obligation to me? Judah wants to build his household, and I'm the one he chose to be the childbearer. Has anything changed?"

Her father's eyes flickered. "If Judah meant to keep his word, he wouldn't have sent you here. He sent you back because he wants to be rid of you. Everyone will know Judah thinks a daughter of my house is the cause of his ill fortune!"

How her father's words stung! Her eyes burned hot with tears.

"Give Judah time to grieve, Father. Give him time to think!"

"Time! All the advantages I gained with your marriage are lost to me! Do you think Judah will bring his flocks to my fields with you here? I'll have to find other shepherds to bring their flocks and herds, or my land will go unnourished." He glowered at her. "You're useless! You're a plague on my house! I have other daughters who need husbands! Will any man offer for the sister of an accursed woman like you? Judah would probably consider it a favor if I killed you!"

The cruel, thoughtless words rained down upon Tamar and hurt her far worse than blows. She quaked inwardly but dared not show weakness. "As you wish, Father. Strike me down. And when Judah sends for me so that his son can have sons, tell him, 'I killed Tamar in a fit of rage!'"

"I'll cast you out the same way he did."

"He sent me home to my father for safekeeping. Will you tell Judah you rejected me? Will you tell this Hebrew warrior that his daughter-in-law was sent away to glean in other men's fields, beg bread, and prostitute herself in order to survive? I'm certain Judah will understand. Hebrews are easily swayed, aren't they? They're given to mercy. They forgive a wrong done to them. My father-in-law will be as merciful to you as you are to me!"

He was listening. Tamar pressed her advantage. "If I'm ruined and made unfit for Shelah, what will happen to Judah's household? I will always be Judah's daughter-in-law. Shelah is Judah's *last* son, Father. Is Judah the sort of man who will let his household die for want of children? He *chose* me!" She paused, giving him a thoughtful look. "Unless you wish to return the bride-price."

Her father paled.

She softened her voice. "Judah has asked a simple thing of you, Father. Give me food, water, and shelter for a time and receive his blessing for it."

"How much time?"

"A few years, perhaps. Whatever time Shelah needs to become man enough to be my husband."

The root of fear had been deeply planted in her father. That fear must be the hedge of protection around her. "You want Judah as an ally, Father, not an enemy. You are not strong enough to stand against him."

He sneered, his eyes cunning. "He is but one man and has but one son now."

A chill washed over her. Had she jeopardized Judah's household by reminding her father of their dwindling numbers? She could see what he was thinking. He had six sons. Her mind raced in Judah's defense. "Judah has many brothers, many fierce brothers. And their father is Jacob, a man who speaks with the unseen, living God who destroyed Sodom and Gomorrah. Don't forget what Jacob's sons did to Shechem. An entire town was destroyed because of the dishonor done one girl. Am I not Judah's daughter now, wife of his firstborn, Er, wife of Onan, promised wife of his last son, Shelah? What will Judah's God do to you if you attempt to destroy his household?"

Zimran paled. He wet his lips nervously. "You will work," he said with bluster. "You won't sit around growing fat and lazy on his promise. You will be a servant in my house until such time as he calls for you."

She bowed her head so that he wouldn't see her relief. "I am your humble servant, Father."

"I had such hope you would build a bridge," he said bitterly. "The stars did not foresee the trouble you would bring me."

Her throat was tight with tears. She swallowed them and

spoke with grave respect. "One day Judah will thank you."

Zimran gave a bitter laugh. "I doubt it, but I'll take no risks over a mere girl. You will sleep with the handmaidens. You're unfit company for your sisters."

Tamar knew he sought to hurt her because she'd failed him. She raised her head and looked at him. He frowned slightly and looked away. "You may go."

She rose from the floor with dignity. "May the God of Judah bless you for your kindness toward me."

His eyes narrowed. "Before you go, there's something I want you to think about." His eyes were hard. "You're young. Soon your widow's garb will chafe you. The years will pass, and you'll see your chances of bearing children fade."

"I will be faithful, Father."

"You say that now, but a time will come when you'll long to remove the sackcloth and ashes and your *tsaiph* of black. But I'm warning you: If you ever do, I'll let Judah decide your fate. We both know what that will be."

Her death, no doubt, followed by celebration.

"I will be faithful. Upon my life, I swear. If it's the last thing I do, I will bring honor upon Judah's house!" Despite the tears flooding her eyes, she lifted her chin and looked into his eyes before she left the room.

+ + +

Judah would have forgotten all about Tamar if Bathshua hadn't become obsessed with finding some way to take vengeance upon the wretched girl. Even after Tamar was gone, his wife gave him no peace.

"My sons must be avenged! As long as she lives, I'll have no rest!"

And neither would he.

Bathshua ceased running the household, leaving her chores to a few lazy servants while she dedicated her days and nights to beseeching her gods for vengeance. She wanted Tamar dead and disaster to befall Zimran's entire household.

"The girl is gone!" Judah shouted in frustration. "Give me some peace and forget about her."

"As you've done!" Accusation reigned. "I have two sons in the grave because of her. If you were any kind of man, you would have killed her! I will never forget what she's done to me! Never!" She returned to her idols, praying to them for vengeance.

Judah left her alone in her misery. Could stone idols hear? Could wood or clay teraphim change anything? Let her find whatever consolation she could.

Judah thought about taking another wife. Another woman might give him more sons, but the thought of another woman under his roof sickened him. He'd grown up in a household with four wives. He knew the trouble women could bring to a man, even women who believed in the same God he did. His father's life had never been easy. Judah's mother and Rachel, his father's favorite wife, had constantly been at odds in their contest to produce sons. Matters only worsened when they both insisted that Jacob take their handmaidens as concubines, each thereby hoping to win the competition. Their sons had been weaned in bitter rivalry. And nothing had ever turned his father's heart from Rachel. Jacob had loved her from the moment he'd first seen her, and her death in childbirth had nearly destroyed him. In truth, he loved her still. He'd loved Joseph and Benjamin more than all the rest of his sons because they had come from Rachel.

No, Judah wouldn't bring more misery upon himself by taking another wife. One woman was enough trouble for any man. Two wives would be double the trouble. He reminded himself often that he'd loved Bathshua once. She was the wife of his youth, the mother of his sons. He wouldn't set her aside for another, no matter how difficult she became.

Besides, he'd have to build another house for fear of what Bathshua would do to any woman he brought into this one. He'd seen her ill treatment of Tamar.

Judah escaped conflict with Bathshua by staying away from his stone house and tending his flocks. He had a justifiable reason for being away for weeks on end. Yet even out in the fields away from his wife, trouble hounded him.

His calves and lambs were cursed by disease or killed by predators. The sun scorched his pasturage. When he kept his animals protected in the wadies so that marauders wouldn't take them, rains came upon the mountains, sending floodwaters through the wadies. Many animals were swept away by a flash flood, their bloated bodies a feast for vultures. When he returned home, he found blight had killed his grapevines. Beetles had devoured his palm tree. The garden had gone fallow for lack of loyal servants. The sky was bronze, the earth iron!

Even Bathshua sickened as the bitter rot of discontent

spread poison through her thinning body. Her face sharpened. Her voice rasped. Her dark eyes became as hard as obsidian. She complained constantly of pain in her neck, her back, her stomach, her bowels. Judah summoned healers, who took his money and left useless potions behind.

Everything Judah had worked twenty years to build was turning to ashes before his eyes. And he knew why.

God is against me!

Lying on the hard ground in the opening of his sheepfold, a stone for a pillow, Judah stared up at the evening sky and remembered the promise God had given his father, Jacob, so many years ago—the same promise God had given to Jacob's father, Abraham. *Land and descendants as numerous as the stars in the heavens!* The Lord had blessed Jacob-Israel with twelve sons.

Judah was haunted by nightmares about the fateful day in Dothan. His own words cursed him. *"What can we gain by killing our brother? Let's sell Joseph to those Ishmaelite traders!"* The dry cistern yawned like a black hole in his dreams, and he could hear the cries of his helpless younger brother.

He knew it was because of what he and his brothers had done to Joseph that his life was now in ruins. There was no way to go back, no way to undo his part in it.

"Help me, brothers! Help me!" Judah remembered the boy struggling against his shackles and sobbing for help from those who should have protected him. *"Help me!"* The boy's sobs still echoed, the same way they had the day he was dragged away to Egypt as his brothers watched.

Judah had shown no mercy to Joseph then.

Judah expected no mercy from God now.

+   +   +

Though outwardly obedient, inwardly Tamar balked at
fate, for it was not her destiny to grow old and die without
having children. Four years passed, but Tamar clung tena-
ciously to hope. She was still young; there was still time.

She worked hard for her father's household. She gave him
no opportunity to complain. She made pottery. She wove
baskets and cloth. She made tools for her brothers and
sisters to use in the fields. Only when the shepherds had
taken their flocks away did her father send her out into
the fields to work. Though the work was grueling, she
preferred the open spaces. Better a burden of rock than the
burden of others' contempt.

Her father prospered. The third year Zimran harvested
twofold from his fields. "Where is the ill fortune you were
sure I would bring you?" she said in challenge.

"Let's wait and see what next year brings."

By the fifth year her father's household prospered so
greatly that everyone forgave her presence. Her sisters
married, and she was welcomed into the house. Her brother
took a wife. Tamar became an object of pity. She would have
welcomed their compassion, but she despised their charity.
They looked down upon her and upon Judah's household.

She held on to her hope. She clung to it. One day Judah
would send for her! One day she would have children!
Someday the house of Judah would be strong and held in
high honor because of the sons she would give them. She
wept, for she ached to take her rightful place as the
childbearer in her husband's clan. What greater dream
could a woman have?

Yet sometimes in the night, when Tamar heard the soft mewling sounds of her brother's firstborn son, she wept. Would she ever hold a child of her own?

Surely Judah had not forsaken her. Surely he would send for her. He had given his promise. Perhaps this year. Perhaps next. Oh, let it be soon!

When she was alone in the fields, Tamar lifted up her eyes to the heavens, tears streaking her face. *How long, oh, Lord, how long will I be abandoned? How long before justice is done? Oh, God of Judah, help me. When will this son of yours see that I can give his household the children he needs so that the name of Judah will not die? Change his heart, God. Change his heart.*

Having prayed to Judah's unseen God, Tamar did the only thing left to her.

She waited . . .

   and waited . . .

      and waited. . . .

five

ON market day, while her father and brothers sat in the
city gate visiting with friends, Tamar remained in the goat-
hair booth with her mother and sold cloth made from the
flax. Sharp-eyed, sharp-tongued patrons never cowed
Tamar, and the booth always showed a good profit when
she managed it. Her mother was content to leave it in her
hands.

Business had been brisk, and Tamar was kept very busy
while her mother sat and stitched the sun, the moon, and
the stars on a red gown she'd made for her daughter in
Timnah. Every year Tamar's sister received a new gown
and veil. Zimran grumbled at the cost of the cloth and
colored thread but never refused to allow his wife to
purchase whatever she needed. Only the best would do for
a temple priestess, and her father coveted the favor of the

gods, any and all of them. Tamar's mother spent hours working with her fine threads and tiny beads, trimming the gowns and exquisite veils she made from imported cloth of red and blue. She also made anklets with rows of tiny bells.

Though Tamar wore her mourning garments until they were threadbare, she never asked for more or wished for the finery her sister was given. Tamar was satisfied with her voluminous black *tsaiph* that covered her from head to foot. The garment didn't chafe, but the barren wasteland of her life did. Despair wore upon her resolve.

She'd been born for more than this! She'd been brought up and trained to be a wife and mother of a household! Six years had come and gone, and still no summons from Judah!

Tamar rose and haggled with another customer. It was late in the day, and the man wanted quality textiles for bargain prices. She refused his price and sat down. He offered more. They haggled again. Finally, the man purchased the last of the cloth and left. With a sigh, Tamar sat inside the booth with her mother.

"I'm going to need more blue thread. I thought I had enough to finish this sash, but I still need more. Go and buy more for me, but be quick about it."

Tamar walked past booths displaying baskets of figs and pomegranates, trays of grapes, jars of olive oil and honey, skins of wine, bowls of spices from Eastern caravans. Children played beside mothers hawking merchandise. Tamar saw other widows, all much older than she, sitting content while grown sons or daughters-in-law conducted the business.

Depressed, she purchased the blue thread her mother

needed and headed back. She walked down a different aisle of booths displaying wood, clay, and stone teraphim; pottery; baskets; and weaponry. She was restless and dejected, when she noticed two men coming toward her. One looked vaguely familiar. She frowned, wondering if he was a friend of her brothers.

As he came closer, she realized it was *Shelah!* Shocked, she stared, for he was a full-grown man boasting a beard and broad shoulders! His companion was a young Canaanite, and both were armed with curved knives. Each had a wineskin draped over his shoulders, and they were both drunk! Shelah swaggered down the narrow lane. He bumped into a man, shoved him aside, and cursed him. Tamar couldn't seem to move. She stood gawking at them, her heart racing.

"Well, look at her, Shelah." His friend laughed. "The poor widow can't take her eyes off of you. Perhaps she wants something from you."

Shelah brushed her aside with scarcely a look and snarled, "Get out of my way."

Heat poured into her face, for Judah's son hadn't even recognized her! He was just like Er, arrogant and contemptuous. He bumped into a counter, rattling the clay teraphim displayed there. The proprietor made a grab for his merchandise as Shelah and his friend laughed and strolled on.

"Get out of my way. . . ."

Tamar fought against the anger and despair filling her. Judah never meant to keep his promise!

What would become of her when her father died? Would she have to beg crumbs from her brothers' tables or go out and glean in a stranger's field? For the rest of her life, she would suffer the shame of abandonment and have to survive on others' pity. All because Judah had forsaken her. *It was not just!* Judah had lied. She was left with nothing. No future! No hope!

Tamar returned to her father's booth and gave the blue thread to her mother. Then she sat in the deepest shadows, her face turned away.

"You were gone a long time. What kept you?"

Hot tears burned Tamar's eyes, but she refused to look at her mother. "The woman was stubborn about the price." She would not expose her shame.

Her mother made no further reprimand, but Tamar felt her watchful eyes. "Is something wrong, Tamar?"

"I'm tired." Tired of this endless waiting. Tired of hoping Judah would keep his promise. Tired of the barrenness of a useless life! She clenched her hands. She needed wise counsel, but whom could she trust? She couldn't speak with her father, for he'd merely tell her he'd been right all along: Judah had cast her out and abandoned her. She couldn't speak with her mother because she was content with things as they were. She was getting older and needed extra hands to help. Her father was wealthy enough now to have servants, but he preferred to sink his profits into a new stone storage house for surplus grain.

The market day ended, and the booths were dismantled. Her father and brothers came in time to load the donkey. It was a long walk home.

Tamar didn't speak of Shelah until she was alone with Acsah.

"Did he speak to you?"

"Oh yes. He told me to get out of his way." Tamar pressed a hand over her mouth, silencing the sob that choked her. She closed her eyes, struggling for control over her emotions. She shook her head.

Acsah embraced her and stroked her back. "I knew this day would come."

"I stood right in front of him, Acsah, and he didn't even know me."

"You were a young girl when you entered Judah's house. Now you're a woman. It's not surprising Shelah didn't recognize you. I doubt even Judah would."

"You don't understand what this means!"

"Yes, I do. You're the one who never understood."

Tamar drew back. "I thought . . ."

Acsah shook her head. "You hoped. You were the only one who had faith in that man." She touched her cheek tenderly. "He is the one who has been faithless." ← Japhthah

"I must do something, Acsah. I can't leave things as they are."

They talked far into the night but came up with no solutions. Finally, exhausted, Tamar fell into a fitful sleep.

✦   ✦   ✦

Tamar was milking the goats when her mother came to her. It was clear something was terribly wrong. She rose. "What's happened, Mother?"

"Judah's wife is dead." Tears slid down her mother's wrinkled cheeks, but her eyes were like fire.

Tamar stepped back, her body going cold. "Who sent word?"

"No one sent word! Your father heard about it from a friend who has commerce with the Hebrews. Judah's wife is already buried! You were not even summoned to mourn her." Her eyes were fierce and black. "That my daughter should be so ill-treated by a Hebrew and nothing be done about it will bring me down to my grave!" She wept bitter tears.

Tamar turned her face away and closed her eyes. She wished she could sink into the earth and be spared this final humiliation.

Her mother came closer. "When will you see your situation for what it is? Your brother saw Shelah in the marketplace. He took pity on you and told me rather than your father! Shelah's a grown man! Perhaps he's left his father's household. Perhaps he'll choose his own wife and do whatever he pleases. Judah did!"

Tamar turned away. What she said was true. Judah had never had control over his sons. He'd never been able to rein in Er or Onan. Why should anything be different with Shelah? All the men of Judah's household lived for the pleasure of the moment without thought of tomorrow! Shaking, Tamar paced. She had to do something or scream. She sat down and went back to milking the goats.

"How can you say nothing at such news? This despicable man has abandoned you!"

"Enough!" Tamar glared up at her mother. "I will not speak against Judah or his sons. I will remain loyal to the house of my husband, no matter how they—or you—treat me." She wished she could control her thoughts as easily as her tongue!

"At least we give you bread."

"Grudgingly. I earn every bite I take."

"Your father says you should go to Kezib and shout at the gate for justice!"

So her father knew everything. Her humiliation was complete. Tamar put her forehead against the side of the goat; her anguish was too deep for tears.

"You should have cried out against Judah long ago." Her mother was relentless. "It's your right! Will you sit here for the rest of your life and do nothing? Who will provide for you when you grow old? What will happen to you when you can no longer work? What will happen to you when you're too old to glean?" She knelt beside Tamar and grasped her arm. "Let the elders know how this Hebrew has treated you and brought shame upon us! Let everyone know that Judah breaks his vow!"

Tamar looked at her. "I know the man better than you, Mother. If I shame him before all Kezib and Adullam, he will not bless me for it! If I blacken the name of my father-in-law, will he show me kindness and mercy and give me Shelah?"

Her mother stood in disgust. "So you will go on waiting. You will accept what he's done to you. You'll let the years pass and grow old without children." Tears came hot and heavy. "How many years will it be before your time of childbearing passes? You won't be young forever! Who will take pity on you when your father dies?"

Tamar covered her face. "Please do not vex me so! I'm searching for a way . . ." She wept.

Her mother said nothing for a long moment. She put her hand gently on Tamar's shoulder. "Life is hard for a woman, Tamar. But it's impossible without a man."

Tamar drew a shaky breath and raised her head. "I know that better than anyone." Rubbing the tears away, she looked at her mother. "I will find a way."

Her mother sighed and looked out toward the hills. "The man who spoke with your father said Judah's wife was ill for a long time. Two years, at least. She must have died a slow, cruel death." She hesitated, her brow furrowed. "Judah had only one wife, didn't he?"

"Only Bathshua."

"No concubines?"

"None." Milk splashed into the earthen bowl as Tamar worked. Focusing on her task, she tried to ignore her mother's gentle touch. It would be her undoing, and she'd cried enough to last a lifetime.

"The man said Judah was going to Timnah with his friend from Adullam," her mother said and let the words hang in the air before adding, "The sheepshearing festival will begin soon."

Tamar looked up at her. Her mother smiled faintly, eyes keen. She said nothing more. Brushing Tamar's shoulder lightly with her fingertips, she left her alone to think.

Mom's Idea?.

And how her thoughts whirled as she worked. Judah might be unwilling to keep his promise, but she still had rights. According to the customs of her people, if Judah wouldn't allow Shelah to sleep with her and give her a son, then Judah himself owed her one.

So Judah was going to the sheepshearing now that his wife was dead! Righteous indignation filled her. Timnah was a center of commerce and the worship of Astarte. She knew what her father-in-law would do there. There were common harlots by the dozens, who sold their bodies for a scrap of bread and a cup of wine! Such might be her own fate if her father cast her out.

She would no longer sit quietly by, waiting for Judah to honor a promise he'd never intended to keep. If she didn't do something soon, Judah would be led by his lusts and carelessly give up his seed—what rightfully belonged to her—to the first woman in Timnah who tantalized him.

Biting her lip, Tamar considered her options. She could continue her chaste existence and wait upon Judah to do what was right, knowing now that he never would, or she could go after him. She could pretend to be a harlot by the roadside. Shelah hadn't recognized her. Why should Judah?

She carried the earthen vessel into the house, where her mother was putting the last touches on her sister's veil. Tamar set the bowl down and looked at the finery lying across her mother's lap. What if she were to dress in her sister's garments?

"This is the best veil I've ever made." Her mother tied off and bit a thread. "There. It's finished." She held it up.

Tamar took the veil from her mother's hand and ran it carefully through her own. "It's very beautiful."

"Look at the gown." Her mother rose and took up the gown for Tamar to see. "I've made everything your sister needs: headband, veils, gown, sash, anklets, and sandals." She turned toward Tamar. "The veil was the last piece." She stretched out her arm, and Tamar laid the veil carefully over it. Tamar noticed that her mother's hands were trembling as she carefully folded the veil and tucked it into the basket. "Your father plans to send these things to your sister in two days. She must have everything in time for the festival."

Did her mother suspect the plan that was forming in her mind? "I'll work in the fields tomorrow, Mother. I may not return to the house until very late."

Her mother tied the basket closed but didn't rise or look at her. "It's a three-hour walk to the crossroads at Enaim. You will have to start out just before dawn."

Tamar's heart lurched, but she said nothing.

Her mother bowed her head. "If Judah recognizes you, he'll kill you. You know that, don't you?"

"If I die, I die."

"Shelah is a shallow young man. He would be easier to fool."

"Perhaps, Mother. But I don't want another jackal. I'm going after the lion."

+ + +

The oil lamp was still burning when Tamar rose in the night. Her mother knew exactly how much oil to use so that the light would last through the heaviest darkness. Soon the lamp would flicker and go out, just in time for the first hint of dawn to light the room. Tamar tiptoed across the room and picked up the basket with her sister's clothing. She left the house with it.

The sun was rising, turning the stars into dying sparks in the paling sky. Tamar walked quickly across her father's fields to the hills beyond. The sun was up and the earth warming by the time she reached the crossroads of Enaim. She entered an olive grove, hurrying into its depths where she would be hidden.

Stripping off her widow's garb, Tamar put on the garments and trappings her mother had made for her priestess sister. She loosened her hair, combing her fingers through the thick, black, curling mass until it hung down her back to below her waist. She put on the veil. The tiny bells around her ankles tinkled as she tucked her black *tsaiph* into the basket and hid it behind a tree.

Grim but determined, Tamar walked back and waited at the edge of the grove where passersby wouldn't see her. She kept watch for the rest of the morning. Her heart leaped into her throat every time she saw two men coming down the road, but she stayed hidden. She would show herself to no men but Judah and his Adullamite friend.

It was well past noon when Judah appeared on the rise with Hirah at his side. She stepped out and sat at the edge of the grove. She rose and stepped forward as they came closer. The anklet bells tingled softly and caught Judah's immediate attention. He slowed his pace and looked at her.

Her palms were slick with sweat, her heart hammering wildly. She wanted to run into the orchard and hide herself again, but she vowed not to lose courage now. She must be bold. Deliberately ignoring the men, she leaned down, lifted the hem of the gown, and adjusted the thin straps of one sandal. The two men stopped.

"We're in no hurry," the Adullamite said, his tone amused.

When she straightened, Tamar didn't look his way. She didn't want him to approach her. She fixed her gaze upon Judah—it was he whose attention she sought. Would he recognize her? Her breath caught tensely as he turned aside and came to her. He stopped right in front of her and smiled, his gaze moving downward. Judah didn't recognize her. He had scarcely looked at her veiled face.

"Here, now," he said, "let me sleep with you."

Tamar was shocked at how easily he fell prey to a woman's wiles, even a woman who was completely inexperienced in the art of seduction! Was this the way men bought the services of a harlot? What should she say now?

"She wants you, Judah." Hirah grinned. "See how she trembles."

"Perhaps she's shy." Judah smiled wryly. "Go on ahead, Hirah. I'll catch up later."

Hirah chuckled. "It's been a long time, hasn't it, my friend!" He walked down the road, leaving Tamar alone with Judah. She almost lost her nerve because of the intensity of his eyes. He never looked away.

"So," he said, "we're alone now. What do you say?"

She could tell his need was great, but no greater than her anger. Would her sister have felt pity? Tamar couldn't muster any. Seven years ago she had begged him not to allow his son Onan to treat her like a harlot! Judah had wanted her to entice his son into doing what was right.

Today she would do so with Judah himself.

She took a step away from him, looking back over her shoulder coyly. "How much will you pay me?" She spoke low, in a tone she hoped would beguile him.

"I'll send you a young goat from my flock."

And where was his flock? Her anger heated. How like Judah to promise something he had no intention of giving. First, a son. Now, a goat! She wouldn't accept another promise from his lips. Not on this day, or any other. "What pledge will you give me so I can be sure you will send it?" She lowered her eyes so he would not see the fire that raged within her. Had he sensed it in her voice or mistaken the tremor for unbridled passion?

Judah stepped closer. "Well, what do you want?"

Tamar considered quickly. She wanted something that bore Judah's name. If she became pregnant, she would need something to prove him responsible. "I want your identification seal, your cord, and the walking stick you're carrying." As soon as she uttered the words, her heart stopped. She had asked for too much! No man in his right mind would agree to give up so much, especially to a harlot! Judah would guess now. He would reach out and rip the veils from her face and kill her right there at the crossroads.

She jerked slightly as he reached out. Then she realized he was handing her his staff! Tamar took it, then watched in amazement as Judah removed the cord from around his neck and handed her his seal as well. He hadn't even uttered a word of protest! The man was driven by lust! *or did he know.*

A bitter sadness gripped Tamar. It took all her willpower not to wail and weep loudly. All the years she had waited for this man to do what was right, and then to find that he thought nothing at all of handing the keys to his household over to a woman he thought was a prostitute!

The sadness ebbed quickly, replaced by excitement. She had cause to hope. Though she had shed her pride and degraded herself, she had this one opportunity to provide a child for the household of Judah. Acsah had said the time was right. She could only hope so.

"Have you a room in town?" Judah said.

"The day is fair, my lord, and grass far softer than a bed of stone." Judah's staff in her hand, she walked into the olive grove. He followed.

+   +   +

Judah took his pleasure beneath the shade of an olive tree and fell asleep in the afternoon heat. Tamar rose quietly and left him there. She hurried through the trees, found the basket she'd hidden, and quickly stripped off her sister's garments and put on her own. Looping Judah's cord and seal around her neck, she tucked them beneath her black mourning garment. She folded the red dress, veils, and sash and put them carefully away, tucking the belled anklets deep into the folds, where they would make no sound.

Hope was alive within her. She pressed her hands over her womb as tears ran down her cheeks. Bowing her head, she whispered softly, "I only ask for justice!"

Judah's sons had abused and used her; Bathshua had blamed her for their sins; and Judah had cast her out, broken his promise, and abandoned her. But now, she might yet be grafted into the line of Abraham, Isaac, and Jacob. Without Judah even knowing, he may have given her a child. If his seed had taken, she might yet have her place among the people whom the God of all creation had chosen to be His own. And if the child were a son, he would be her deliverer.

Tamar reverently touched the seal hidden beneath her garment. She picked up the basket and tucked it under her arm. She took Judah's staff from where it rested against an olive tree and headed home.

+ + +

A spear of light touched Judah's eyelids and awakened him. The harlot was gone. When he didn't find her standing alongside the road where he'd first seen her, he assumed she'd gone into town. Grim and uneasy, he went on with his journey, spending the rest of the day in regret. He was no better than Esau, who had given away his birthright for a bowl of lentil stew! Why had he agreed to hand over his staff, seal, and cord to a temple prostitute? Having taken his pleasure, he found himself impatient to have his possessions in hand again.

Annoyed, he caught up with Hirah near Timnah. His friend irritated him further with taunts and salacious comments.

"Where's your staff, Judah? Don't tell me . . ."

"I'll have it back when I send a goat to the woman."

"And your seal and cord as well?" Hirah laughed and slapped him on the back. "I hope she was worth the price!"

Ashamed, Judah gave no response. He made excuses and went to find Shelah, who had been sent ahead with the flocks. They sheared the sheep together. Judah made contracts with several farmers to bring his sheep after the harvest. Hirah joined them but refrained from further remarks about the harlot by the roadside. "Come, my friend, relax and enjoy yourself," Hirah said, swaying from too much drink. "You have nothing to worry about. Life sorts itself out. Remember how we lived before wives and sons and worries. Timnah has much to offer."

Shelah was eager to try everything. Judah found he couldn't. He kept remembering what an hour of pleasure had already cost him. He missed the feel of his staff in his hand and knew he wouldn't feel right until he had his seal and cord back as well. He was ready to leave long before the festival was over. When it was, he found he couldn't bring himself to follow the same road home again. He made excuses to Hirah.

"I need to take my flocks to better forage. You're going back by way of Enaim, aren't you?"

"As I always do."

"I've done many favors for you, have I not, Hirah? Take this goat back to the harlot by the crossroads of Enaim. Retrieve my staff, seal, and cord from the prostitute and bring them to me at my house. Do that for me, my friend, and I will show my appreciation when next I see you!"

Hirah's eyes gleamed. "Of course."

"One more thing I ask of you."

Hirah lifted his hand. "You needn't say another word, Judah. You're my friend. No one will hear a word of this from my lips." He grinned. "Besides, it will be my pleasure to do your bidding." He headed off down the road, tossing back over his shoulder, "Perhaps I'll pass a few hours in that olive grove myself!"

Judah thought no more about the girl or the cost of his sin until weeks later, when Hirah passed by his house empty-handed. "I made a thorough search for the girl, Judah. I even went into the town, but everyone said there had never been a temple prostitute at the crossroads. They laughed and asked me why I'd think there would be one there when the temple is in Timnah."

Judah had never considered why a temple prostitute

would loiter by the road. Now that he thought about it, he wondered why he hadn't! Confused, Judah became angry, convinced he'd been tricked somehow but having no idea of the reason. Why would the harlot lie to him? Of what possible use were his cord, seal, and staff to a prostitute? A goat could be sold and then the money used for sustenance. Who would buy a seal and staff that bore another man's name, especially a name as well known as his?

"What do you want me to do, Judah?" Hirah sipped his wine. "Shall we both go back and search for her again?"

"Let her keep the pledges! We tried our best to send her the goat. We'd be the laughingstock of the village if we went back again."

When Hirah departed a few days later, Judah went out and cut a straight, strong branch from an almond tree. He whittled the bark and carved his name into the wood. The new staff was a good one, but it didn't have the feel of the one his father had placed in his hands. Nor did the clay seal he made have the same feel of authenticity that his stone seal had had.

But after that, Judah forgot entirely the incident at the crossroads of Enaim.

six

TAMAR said nothing about her successful journey to Enaim, and her mother didn't ask about it. The following morning, Zimran left for Timnah with Tamar's older brother. They took the basket containing the temple garb with them.

When two weeks passed and there was no show of blood, Tamar knew she was pregnant. She was exultant as well as terrified. She kept her secret and went on as always. She rose early and worked all day. No one noticed any change in her, though Acsah was hardest to convince and perplexed by her sudden modesty.

At night, while the others slept, Tamar would spread her hands over her womb. Sometimes her fear would rise, and she would wonder how she had ever dared to trick Judah. What would he do when he found out? She'd been willing

to risk everything, even her life, for the chance to bear a
child. Now she was afraid for the child she carried. Soon
her pregnancy would become apparent, if Acsah hadn't
guessed already. If her father learned of it, he might kill her
in a fit of rage. If she died, so too would Judah's child—and
Judah's line would be lost.

She tried to think clearly and not allow her emotions to
run wild. She was still a part of Judah's household, whether
he acknowledged her or not. The decision of whether she
lived or died must be his, not her father's. Truth was her
only protection, but she couldn't reveal it in a way that
would bring shame upon Judah. Had she wanted to do that,
she would have cried out before the city gates long before
this.

She kept her secret, refusing even to confide in Acsah,
who plagued her daily with questions. "Where were you
that day? Why didn't you awaken me? I searched for you
in the fields. Tell me where you went and why."

Finally Acsah challenged her in private. "What have you
done, Tamar? Who have you lain with? By the gods, we're
both undone!"

"I did what I had to do, Acsah. It's the law of both
Judah's people and mine that I have the right to a child by
Shelah or by Judah himself. And yet I've had to risk everything to receive justice at Judah's hands. I have shamed
myself and resorted to trickery to beget this child, lest I die
in disgrace." She grasped her nurse's hands and held them
tightly. "You must trust me."

"You must speak out and tell—"

"No. Nothing can be said. Not yet."

"And when your father finds out? Will he have mercy on you when he thinks you've committed adultery?"

"It will be up to Judah to decide what happens to me."

"Then you'll die, and the child will die with you. Judah thinks you bring ill fortune and are the cause of his sons' deaths. This will give him an excuse to be rid of you!"

"Speak no more of it."

"Your father will kill you when he finds out!" Acsah closed her eyes and covered her face. "You should have waited."

"I would have grown old and died before Judah called for me."

"And so you destroy yourself and a child with you? You've betrayed Judah and brought shame upon this house. Tell me what happened."

"I will tell you nothing." Caution and hope for a brighter future kept her silent.

This was her secret and Judah's, though the man wasn't even aware of it yet. She would guard this knowledge and keep it private, for it was precious. Judah's staff was beneath her pallet, and the cord and seal ring were still around her neck, hidden by her widow's garb. She wouldn't show them to Acsah. She wouldn't wag her tongue and give her nurse or her father cause to laugh at Judah. She wanted to fulfill her duty to his household. She wanted to be embraced by his people. Would Judah thank her if she exposed him to ridicule?

Loyalty,

Tamar thought of Judah's pride, his pain, his losses. She wouldn't add humiliation to his sorrow. Judah had forsaken her, but she would not shame the father of her child before any man or woman.

The morning she had walked over her father's fields and stood near the crossroads waiting for Judah, she'd had time to think long and hard about the risk she was taking and what the future might hold. Life or death, Judah would decide. When she had stood over Judah as he slept, she'd trembled with anger. She'd almost kicked him awake and confronted him with his sin. She had longed to shake him and cry out: "See what you've brought me to, Judah! See what you've done!" He had once told her to play the harlot for Onan. Instead, she'd played the part for him.

But she had let her anger go. She didn't want revenge. She wanted justice. She was gambling everything in the hope of something better, something important, something permanent. A child. A reason to live! A future and a hope! She fanned the tiny flame growing within her, even knowing everything was still in Judah's hands.

"Perhaps you'll be fortunate and miscarry," Acsah said.

"If that happens, may I die with my child."

"You may die before that." Acsah covered her face and wept.

Tamar smiled sadly. What caused her to hope so much in a man who had never done anything right in all the time she'd known him? Had Judah protected her from Er's brutality or seen that Onan fulfilled his duty to his brother? Judah himself had broken his promise to give her Shelah. How could she hope to survive when her life was in the hands of this man?

And yet, she did hope. She chose to hope. She refused to give in to the fears that gripped her, fear for the child she carried—Judah's child, Judah's hope, Judah's future.

But would the man listen when the time came for her to reveal the truth?

+ + +

Two more months passed before the day of wrath and judgment fell upon Tamar's head. Acsah shook her awake. Disoriented, Tamar sat up. She realized she'd fallen asleep by the stone wall where she'd been working.

"You're undone," Acsah said, tears streaking her face. "Undone! A servant saw you sleeping and went to your father. He summoned me. I had to tell him. I had to." She gripped Tamar's arms tightly. "Run away, Tamar. You must hide yourself!"

A strange calmness filled Tamar. Her waiting was over. "No," she said quietly and rose. Two brothers were striding across the field toward her. Let them come. When they reached her, they cursed her with foul accusations. She said nothing as they grabbed her arms and headed back. Her father came outside, his face red, hands in fists.

"Are you with child?"

"Yes."

Zimran didn't ask who the father was before he flew at her. The first blow knocked her down. When he kicked at her, she scrambled away and rolled into a ball so that he couldn't harm the baby. "It's not your right to pass judgment on me!" She screamed at him in fury equal to his own.

"Isn't it? You're my daughter!" He kicked her again.

Gasping for breath, she started to rise, but he grabbed her shawl and the braid of hair beneath it, dragging her up and back. She clawed his hands to get free. She had the lion's cub in her womb, and she would fight like a lioness to save it. She stood, feet planted, hands raised. "I belong to Judah's household, not yours! Or have you forgotten?"

"He'll thank me for killing you!"

"Judah must be the one to pass judgment! Not you! Judah and no other!"

Breathing hard, Zimran stared at her. "You've played the harlot beneath my nose! I should kill you!"

Tamar saw the tears of rage and shame in her father's eyes, but she wouldn't weaken. "Why save Judah the trouble, Father? Why have my blood on your hands? He abandoned me six years ago! Let it be on his head what happens to me and my child."

Her father shouted for a servant. "Go and tell Judah: Tamar is pregnant by harlotry! Ask him what he wants done with her!" The servant ran across the field. Zimran glared at her. "As for you, harlot, go and wait."

Tamar obeyed. Alone, she trembled violently. She clenched her hands, her palms damp with sweat. Her heart quaked.

What if Judah didn't come?

✦   ✦   ✦

The news of Tamar's harlotry and her pregnancy rocked Judah and enraged him. Though it had been six years since he'd removed her from his house, he expected her to remain chaste for as long as she lived. If he showed Tamar any mercy and allowed her to live, the child, no matter who the father was, would become part of his household. He couldn't let that happen. He wouldn't.

Mingled with his wrath was elation. Tamar had given him an opportunity to get rid of her. She had sinned against his house in the vilest way, and it was his right to judge her. Bathshua would have been exultant. She had been right after all: Tamar was no good. The girl was evil. She had cost him Er and Onan! The wisest thing he'd ever done was withhold Shelah.

Let her suffer. Hadn't he suffered because of her? Stoning was too swift, too easy. Let her feel the pain of her transgressions against him. "Bring her out and burn her! Burn her, I say!" Judah shouted.

Before Zimran's servant was out the door, Judah felt certain his fortune had changed. By tomorrow, the time would be ripe to find a suitable wife for his last son, Shelah. It was time now to build up his household.

✦   ✦   ✦

Tamar heard the commotion and knew what Judah had decided. Her mother was wailing, her father shouting. She covered her face and prayed. *God of heaven and earth, help me! I know I'm not of Your people. I know I'm unworthy. But if You care about Judah, who is Your son, save me! Save this child I carry!*

Acsah hurried into the room. "Judah said to burn you. Oh, Tamar . . ."

Tamar didn't weep or plead. She rose quickly and yanked back the pallet. Removing her shawl, she wrapped Judah's staff in it. She took the cord and seal from around her neck and pressed them into Acsah's hand. "Take these things to Judah. Go quickly, Acsah. Tell him, 'The man who owns this identification seal and walking stick is the father of my child. Do you recognize them?'"

A commotion had started outside. Her mother was pleading

hysterically as her father shouted, *"I warned her! I told her what would happen if she ever took off her widow's garb!"*

"No, you can't—"

"Get out of the way, woman! Tamar brought this upon herself!"

Tamar pushed her nurse. "Go, Acsah! Do not fail me! *Run, woman! Run!*"

As soon as she obeyed, Tamar positioned herself in the corner of the room where she could best defend herself. Her brothers entered. "Will you show no mercy to your own sister?"

"After you've shamed us?" They called her names as they grappled with her. She did not make it easy for them. They dragged her away from the wall and dragged her through the doorway.

Her father stood outside. "Judah said to burn you, and burn you shall!"

Did they think she would die easily? Did they think she wouldn't fight for the life of her unborn child? Tamar kicked and clawed. She bit and screamed at them. "Then let Judah burn me!" They struck her, and with all her pent-up fury, Tamar hit back. "Let him see his judgment carried out! *Take me to Judah!* Why should my death be upon your heads?" She used her fingernails and feet. "Let him be the one to put the torch to me!"

+ + +

Judah saw a woman running toward him, a bundle in her hand. Frowning, he shielded his eyes from the sun's glare and recognized Acsah, Tamar's nurse. Gritting his teeth, he swore under his breath. No doubt she had come to plead for mercy for that wretched girl.

Gasping for breath and shaking with exhaustion, Acsah fell to her knees. She dropped the bundle at his feet. "Tamar sent me . . ." Unable to say more, she grabbed the edge of a black shawl and yanked it hard. A staff rolled out—his staff. She held out her hand and opened it, showing him a red cord with a stone seal.

Judah snatched it from her. "Where did you get these?"

"Tamar . . ."

"Speak up, woman!"

"Tamar! 'Take these things to Judah,' she said. 'The man who owns this identification seal and walking stick is the father of my child. Do you recognize them?'" She bowed her head, fighting for breath.

A sick feeling gripped Judah. He went cold as he picked up his staff. The harlot by the roadside had been Tamar! She'd disguised herself and tricked him into fulfilling her rights to a child. He was awash with shame. Nothing he'd ever done had been unseen. He'd kept nothing secret from the Lord. His skin prickled. His hair raised on end.

"When will you do what is right, Judah?"

The words came like a whisper. Tamar had said these words to him years ago, but it was another voice now, soft and terrifying, that spoke into the recesses of his mind and heart. He gripped his head, trembling inwardly. He shook with fear.

"My lord?" Acsah's eyes were wide.

His heart pumped frantically. He cried out and ran. He had to stop the judgment he'd set in motion. If he didn't reach Zimran in time, two more lives would be upon his head: Tamar's life and the child she carried. *His* child!

"Oh, God, forgive me!" He pushed himself harder, running faster than he'd ever run in his life. "Let the sin be upon my head!" Why hadn't he run like this after the Ishmaelites? Why hadn't he rescued his brother from their hands? It was too late now to undo what he'd done then. *Oh, God, have mercy, God of my father, Israel! Give me strength! Let her life be spared, and the child with her.*

Zimran and his sons were coming to meet him. They were half dragging Tamar, and she was fighting like a mad woman. A brother kicked her as Zimran grabbed her by the hair. Yanking her to her feet, Zimran shoved her toward Judah, cursing her with his every breath.

"Let her go!" Judah shouted. When Zimran hit Tamar again, rage fired Judah's blood. "Strike her again and I'll kill you!"

Zimran was quick to defend himself. "You're the one who told us you wanted her burned! And you've every right. She's betrayed you and played the harlot."

Tamar stood silent now, covered with dust, her face bruised and bleeding. She'd been beaten, dragged, struck, and mocked for *his* sin. Not even her own father and brothers cared enough to show her the least compassion. She stood and said nothing.

Judah's face filled with heat. When had he ever shown this young woman any pity? She'd suffered abuse from Er, and he'd done nothing to stop it. She'd asked for her rights from Onan, and he'd told her to play the harlot. She'd pleaded for justice, and he'd abandoned her. Not once had she cried out before the city gates and embarrassed him. Instead, she'd humbled herself and dressed as a harlot in order to beget a child for his household. And then, rather than expose his sin, she had returned his staff, cord, and seal privately, protecting his reputation.

Tears filled his eyes. His throat closed. She stood before him, battered and bleeding, head bowed, uttering not a word of self-defense, waiting, still waiting, as she'd always waited for him to be the man he should be.

"When will you do what is right, Judah?"

"She is more in the right than I am because I didn't keep my promise to let her marry my son Shelah."

"That may be, but she has no right to play the harlot under my roof!"

Judah looked into the Canaanite's dark eyes and saw a reflection of his own cold heart. Zimran's pride was hurt, and he intended to destroy Tamar for it. Judah's pride broke. Hadn't he blamed Tamar for the sins of others? Without a twinge of conscience, he had rejected and abandoned her. Only a short while ago, he'd felt exultant at the thought of passing judgment upon her and knowing she'd die an agonizing death by fire. He'd sinned against her a hundred times over and in the full sight of God and never once cared about the cost to her. And now that his sins had caught up with him, he had a choice: Go on sinning or repent.

Tamar lifted her head and looked at him. He saw something flash in her eyes. She could expose him right now. She could pour humiliation upon him unendingly. She could tell how she'd tricked him at the crossroads of Enaim, and make him a laughingstock before her father and brothers and everyone else they might tell about it. Judah knew he deserved public ridicule and worse. He saw her anger, her frustration, her grief. And he understood it. But it didn't change his mind.

Judah stepped forward and brought his staff up. He held it in both hands, ready to fight. "Take your hands off her, Zimran. The child is mine." When he took another step forward, Zimran's face went pale. The Canaanite stepped back, his sons with him.

"Take her then. Do with her whatever you want." Zimran strode away with a bemused glance over his shoulder. His sons followed him.

Tamar let out her breath and sank to her knees. Bowing her head, she put her hands on his dirty feet. "Forgive me, my lord." Her shoulders shook and she began to sob.

Judah's eyes filled with tears. He went down on one knee and put his hand gently on her back. "It is I who need your forgiveness, Tamar." The sound of her weeping broke his heart. He helped Tamar to her feet. She was shaking violently. One eye was blackened and swelling. Her lip was bleeding. Her clothes were torn, and scratches showed where she had been dragged across rocky ground.

All those years ago when he'd first seen her in Zimran's field, he'd sensed something about this girl and wanted her for his household. Tamar was a Canaanite, but she was honorable and loyal. She had great courage and strength. Surely it had been God who had led him to choose this girl. She had risked everything to have the child who might preserve his household from complete ruin. He cupped her face. "May the God of my father, Israel, forgive my sins against you!" He kissed her forehead.

Her body relaxed. "And mine against you." She smiled, and her eyes glistened with tears.

Judah felt a deep tenderness toward her. He walked beside her until she stumbled and then swept her up in his arms and carried her the rest of the way home. Acsah ran to meet them, ready to tend Tamar's injuries.

Judah waited outside his stone house, his head in his hands. Pride broken, heart humbled, he prayed as he'd never prayed before, pleading for someone other than himself. It was dusk when Acsah finally came out to him. "How is she?"

"Sleeping, my lord." Acsah smiled. "All seems well."

Tamar hadn't lost his child.

"Praise be to God." He went out among his flock and selected the best he could find—a flawless male lamb. He confessed his sins before the Lord and spilled the blood of the lamb as atonement. Then he prostrated himself before the God of Abraham, Isaac, and Jacob and beseeched Him for forgiveness and restoration.

That night Judah slept without nightmares, for the first time in more years than he could count.

✦ ✦ ✦

Acsah felt as though she were living on the edge of a cliff and could slip over at any moment. Tamar had changed greatly. She had taken command of the house like a first wife would, and her first order was to have all of Bathshua's teraphim removed and destroyed. Shelah joined in protesting, but Judah was adamant in his support of Tamar. Acsah pleaded with Tamar, but it was no use. So she poured out libations in secret, praying to the gods of Canaan that she had managed to hide in her basket. Daily she did this out of devotion and love for Tamar, but when Tamar discovered her in the midst of the ritual, she erupted.

"If you won't obey me, then keep your idols and go back to my father's house with them!"

"I'm only trying to help you," Acsah pleaded, weeping. "Please heed the ways of the past. It is for you and the child that I make contracts with the divine assembly!"

"Our way was wrong, Acsah. I am done with the old ways. If you insist on keeping them, you must leave!"

When Tamar took the clay idol and smashed it against the wall, Acsah cried out in fear. "Do you want the spirits to come against you?"

"This child belongs to Judah and to the God of his people. No other gods will be invited to assemble in Judah's house ever again. If I find you pouring out libations to Baal, I'll send you away!" Tamar reached out for Acsah, weeping. "Do not make me do it, Acsah. I love you, but we will bow down to the God of Israel and no other!"

Acsah had never seen the girl's eyes so fierce. Convinced that the early stress of Tamar's pregnancy had affected her senses, she went to Judah for help. Surely he would want to make sure all the deities were placated and his child protected! But Judah surprised her.

"There will be no other gods in my house. Do as Tamar says."

Frustrated, Acsah obeyed. She spent the months watching over every aspect of Tamar's physical health. She prepared Tamar's meals and told her when to rest. She massaged Tamar's womb and felt the first kick of the baby. She shared Tamar's joy, for she loved the girl as well as the child she carried. She would sit and watch Tamar stroke her growing belly with an expression of love and amazement on her glowing face. Tamar was at peace, and Acsah found herself praying that the unseen God would show mercy upon Tamar and upon the child Tamar had risked everything to conceive.

As the time grew near for Tamar to give birth, Acsah asked if she could build a birthing hut. "Yes," Tamar said, "but do not go by the old ways. Promise me!"

Acsah promised and kept her word. She built the hut herself. She swept the earthen floor and lined it with rush mats, but she didn't chant or sing to the demons. She didn't caulk every opening to keep the spirits out. Instead, she offered prayers to Judah's God, for this was Judah's child.

God of Judah, protect Tamar. Watch over this birth, and bless this girl who has turned away from everything she ever learned so that she could be among Judah's people. I beseech you out of love for her. Show her mercy. Let this child she carries be a son who will love her and care for her in her old age. Let him be a son who will rise up in strength and honor.

It was a difficult birth. Acsah half expected it to be, after her ministrations to Tamar revealed the wondrous news that Tamar's womb held not one, but two, heirs to Judah's line.

Acsah had acted as midwife many times in the household of Zimran, but never once had she witnessed a birth as hard as this one. She loved Tamar even more fiercely, for though the girl suffered greatly, she did not complain. Hour upon hour, Tamar strained, sweat pouring from her. She bit down upon a leather strap to keep from screaming.

"Cry out, Tamar! It will help!"

"Judah will hear and be distressed."

"He's the cause of your pain! Let him hear! I'm sure Bathshua screamed!"

"I am *not* Bathshua!" Tears came as the cords in her neck stood out. "Sing to the Lord God, Acsah." She groaned as the pains took hold of her again. Blood and water soaked the birthing rock on which Tamar sat.

And Acsah did sing, desperately. "I will proclaim the name of the Lord! I will proclaim His name and ascribe greatness to Judah's God, the God of Jacob, the God of Isaac and Abraham."

"His ways are just." Tamar gasped for air and then groaned again, her hands drawing up her knees as she bore down.

The first child's hand came forth, and Acsah quickly tied a scarlet cord around the baby's wrist. "This one came out first," she announced.

"Oh, God, have mercy!" Tamar cried out then, and the child withdrew its hand. She ground her teeth and bore down again. Acsah prayed feverishly as she laid hands upon Tamar's abdomen and felt the two babies struggling within her. They moved, rolled, pressed. Tamar cried out again, and the first child came forth, pushing down and sliding free into Acsah's waiting hands.

"A son!" Acsah laughed with joy, then gasped in surprise. "What!" It was not the child with the scarlet cord upon his wrist. "How did you break out first? He shall be called Perez," she said, for it meant "breaking out."

Within a few moments, the second child was born, another son who was named for the thread soaked in blood—Zerah, meaning "scarlet"—which proclaimed him firstborn, though he had come second.

Tamar smiled wearily. When the afterbirth came, she lay back on the rush-covered earth and closed her eyes with a sigh. "Sons," she said softly and smiled.

Acsah cut the cords, washed the boys, salted and swaddled them, and placed them in their mother's arms. Tamar smiled as she looked from Zerah to Perez. "Do you see what the Lord has done, Acsah? He has lifted the poor in spirit. He has taken me up from the dust and ash heap and given me sons!" Eyes shining with joy, Tamar laughed.

✦   ✦   ✦

Judah couldn't speak when he saw Tamar with two babies in her arms. His emotions were so powerful they choked him. Despite his sins, God had given him a double blessing through this courageous young Canaanite woman. He looked at his two sons and their mother, still pale from her travail, and realized he loved Tamar for the woman she was. He not only loved her, he respected and admired her. When Judah had brought her home to Er, he'd never realized how God would use her to bring him to repentance, to change his heart, to change the direction of his life. Tamar was a woman of excellence, a woman worthy of praise!

She looked at him steadily. "I want my sons to be men of God, Judah. I want you to do to them whatever God requires of you so that they will be counted among His people."

"In eight days I will circumcise my sons, and as soon as you're well enough to travel, we'll leave this place and return to the tents of my father."

Judah watched a trickle of tears seep into the dark hair at her temples. Her eyes were filled with uncertainty, and he guessed why. She had never received tender treatment from Bathshua or his sons. "My father, Jacob, will welcome you, Tamar, and my mother will love you. She'll understand you and what happened between us better than anyone." Tamar was still young, still vulnerable. No woman had ever been more beautiful to him than she was now, precious beyond measure. He would make her way smooth.

She raised her eyes. "How can you be sure your mother will accept me?"

"My mother went to my father in veils."

Her dark eyes flickered in surprise. "Dressed as a harlot?"

"Dressed as a bride, but not the one he wanted." He smiled ruefully. "Still, my father came to love her in his own way. She bore him sons. I'm the fourth of six." Judah saw the pulse beat strongly in Tamar's throat. She looked deeply troubled. It was a moment before he realized why, and the heat rushed into his face. He took her hand and covered it with his own. "Don't misunderstand me, Tamar, or be afraid of our future together. I will show you the respect a man should have for a wife, but you are my daughter now. I won't do as the Canaanites do. I promise." He grimaced, his smile tender and apologetic. "A promise I mean to keep!"

Her dark eyes shone. "I trust you, Judah. You will do what is right."

Bathed in forgiveness, his throat closed. He gently took her hand and kissed her palm.

IN the years ahead, Judah was a different man. He renewed his relationship with his father and reasserted himself as leader over his brothers. He led them to Egypt to buy grain so that Jacob's household could survive the famine that had come upon the land. It was then that God brought him face-to-face with the brother he had forsaken: Joseph.

Unrecognized as Zaphenath-paneah, the pharaoh's overseer, Joseph tested them. When he demanded that Rachel's last son, Benjamin, be left as his slave, Judah stepped forward, claimed the disaster upon them was due to their own sins, and offered his life in place of his brother's. Seeing the change in Judah, Joseph wept and revealed his true identity. He'd long since forgiven them, but now he embraced them. Joseph sent Judah and his brothers back to

Canaan with instructions to bring Jacob and his entire household back to Egypt, where they would claim the rich land of Goshen.

Tamar returned with Judah, her sons grown with sons of their own.

On his deathbed, Jacob-Israel gathered his sons around him and gave them each a blessing. Judah received the greatest one of all. The scepter would never leave his hands. From him and the sons Tamar had borne to him would come the Promised One, God's anointed—the Messiah!

To his last day upon this earth, Judah kept his promise to Tamar. Though he loved her, he never slept with her again. Nor any other woman.

DEAR READER,

You have just read the story of Tamar as perceived by one author. Is this the whole truth about the story of Tamar and Judah? Jesus said to seek and you will find the answers you need for life. The best way to find the truth is to look for yourself!

This "Seek and Find" section is designed to help you discover the story of Tamar as recorded in the Bible. It consists of six short studies that you can do on your own or with a small discussion group.

You may be surprised to learn that this ancient story will have applications for your life today. No matter where we live or in what century, God's Word is truth. It is as relevant today as it was yesterday. In it we find a future and a hope.

Peggy Lynch

l e a d i n g　　h o m e

SEEK GOD'S WORD FOR TRUTH
Go back and read the Bible passage quoted in "Setting the Scene"
on pages ix–xii.

What part did Judah play in this sibling rivalry story?

What did he and his brothers tell their father?

Based on this passage, list some possible reasons that Judah chose to leave his family at "about this time."

Have you ever felt ashamed of some careless act you did that affected others? Were you fearful of being found out? What choices did you make?

Judah had choices. What could he have done differently?

Proverbs 28:13 tells us, "People who cover over their sins will not prosper. But if they confess and forsake them, they will receive mercy."

Had Judah confessed to God and to his father, the story would have ended there. However, he did not. Instead, he got married! It would seem that Judah was on a pathway of separation from truth. He chose to run and hide rather than confront the real issues. He chose to handle things for himself rather than let God direct his path.

FIND GOD'S WAYS FOR YOU

What have you learned about Judah so far? Would you consider him confrontational or passive? Why?

In what ways do you identify with Judah?

How do you deal with jealousy? with conflict?

Where do you turn with life's struggles—to yourself? to family and friends? to comfortable patterns? to God?

STOP AND PONDER

> People who cover over their sins will not prosper. But if
> they confess and forsake them, they will receive mercy.
>
> PROVERBS 28:13

Take a moment to ask God to search your heart. Be quiet before
Him. Reflect on what He offers here.

family ties

SEEK GOD'S WORD FOR TRUTH
Read the following passages:

About this time, Judah left home and moved to Adullam, where he visited a man named Hirah. There he met a Canaanite woman, the daughter of Shua, and he married her. She became pregnant and had a son, and Judah named the boy Er. Then Judah's wife had another son, and she named him Onan. And when she had a third son, she named him Shelah. At the time of Shelah's birth, they were living at Kezib.

When his oldest son, Er, grew up, Judah arranged his marriage to a young woman named Tamar. But Er was a wicked man in the Lord's sight, so the Lord took his life. Then Judah said to Er's brother Onan, "You must marry Tamar, as our law requires of the brother of a man who has died. Her first son from you will be your brother's heir."

But Onan was not willing to have a child who would not be his own heir. So whenever he had intercourse with Tamar, he spilled the semen on the ground to keep her from having a baby who would belong to his brother. But the Lord considered it a wicked thing for Onan to deny a child to his dead brother. So the Lord took Onan's life, too.

Then Judah told Tamar, his daughter-in-law, not to marry again at that time but to return to her parents' home. She was to remain a widow until his youngest son, Shelah, was old enough to marry her. (But Judah didn't really intend to do this because he was afraid Shelah would also die, like his two brothers.) So Tamar went home to her parents.   GENESIS 38:1-11

Shem, Ham, and Japheth, the three sons of Noah, survived the Flood with their father. (Ham is the ancestor of the Canaanites.) From these three sons of Noah came all the people now scattered across the earth.

After the Flood, Noah became a farmer and planted a vineyard. One day he became drunk on some wine he had made and lay naked in his tent. Ham, the father of Canaan, saw that his father was naked and went outside and told his brothers. Shem and Japheth took a robe, held it over their shoulders, walked backward into the tent, and covered their father's naked body. As they did this, they looked the other way so they wouldn't see him naked. When Noah woke up from his drunken stupor, he learned what Ham, his youngest son, had done. Then he cursed the descendants of Canaan, the son of Ham:

"A curse on the Canaanites! May they be the lowest of servants to the descendants of Shem and Japheth." Then Noah said, "May Shem be blessed by the Lord my God; and may Canaan be his servant. May God enlarge the territory of Japheth, and may he share the prosperity of Shem; and let Canaan be his servant."   GENESIS 9:18-27

According to the second passage, who was the father of the Canaanites?

Abraham found a wife for his son Isaac from afar—not a Canaanite. Esau displeased his father, Isaac, by marrying not one, but two, Canaanite women. Isaac sent his son Jacob far away to get a wife who was not a Canaanite.

How did Jacob's son Judah acquire a wife?

Who helped him? Who were her people?

Their firstborn child was a son. Judah named him Er. Who named Onan and Shelah?

What kind of son was Er?

According to the following passage, what does God hate?

> There are six things the Lord hates—no, seven things he detests: haughty eyes, a lying tongue, hands that kill the innocent, a heart that plots evil, feet that race to do wrong, a false witness who pours out lies, a person who sows discord among brothers.   PROVERBS 6:16-19

We read above that "Er was a wicked man." The Hebrew word here translated as *wicked* is also used in numerous other Bible passages. In Genesis 13, Sodom and Gomorrah were called wicked for their practice of sodomy; in the book of Esther, Haman is called wicked for plotting to exterminate the Jews; in Deuteronomy, anyone leading God's people to worship false gods was called wicked.

What did God do to Er?

What might be the reason for Er's death?

What kind of man does God declare Onan to be?

How did Onan displease God? What did God do to him?

Judah's remaining son, Shelah, should have been given to Tamar, according to marriage customs of the times. What reason did Judah give Tamar for delaying the marriage?

What was the real reason?

FIND GOD'S WAYS FOR YOU

Judah was grieving over the past as well as the present, and he was gripped with fear of the future. What fears grip you?

How do you deal with fear?

Er and Onan did their own thing, and it led to death. As the book of Proverbs tells us, "There is a path before each person that seems right, but it ends in death" (Proverbs 14:12). In contrast, Jesus said, "My purpose is to give life in all its fullness" (John 10:10).

Do you know the One who gives life in all its fullness?

STOP AND PONDER

> Jesus said, "I am the way, the truth, and the life. No one can come to the Father except through me"; "Look! Here I stand at the door and knock. If you hear me calling and open the door, I will come in, and we will share a meal as friends." JOHN 14:6; REVELATION 3:20

Will you accept His invitation?

the bride

Read the following passage:

> But Er was a wicked man in the Lord's sight, so the Lord took his life. Then Judah said to Er's brother Onan, "You must marry Tamar, as our law requires of the brother of a man who has died. Her first son from you will be your brother's heir."
>
> But Onan was not willing to have a child who would not be his own heir. So whenever he had intercourse with Tamar, he spilled the semen on the ground to keep her from having a baby who would belong to his brother. But the Lord considered it a wicked thing for Onan to deny a child to his dead brother. So the Lord took Onan's life, too.
>
> Then Judah told Tamar, his daughter-in-law, not to marry again at that time but to return to her parents'

home. She was to remain a widow until his youngest son, Shelah, was old enough to marry her. (But Judah didn't really intend to do this because he was afraid Shelah would also die, like his two brothers.) So Tamar went home to her parents.

In the course of time Judah's wife died. After the time of mourning was over, Judah and his friend Hirah the Adullamite went to Timnah to supervise the shearing of his sheep. Someone told Tamar that her father-in-law had left for the sheep-shearing at Timnah. Tamar was aware that Shelah had grown up, but they had not called her to come and marry him. So she changed out of her widow's clothing and covered herself with a veil to disguise herself. Then she sat beside the road at the entrance to the village of Enaim, which is on the way to Timnah. Judah noticed her as he went by and thought she was a prostitute, since her face was veiled. So he stopped and propositioned her to sleep with him, not realizing that she was his own daughter-in-law.

"How much will you pay me?" Tamar asked.

"I'll send you a young goat from my flock," Judah promised.

"What pledge will you give me so I can be sure you will send it?" she asked.

"Well, what do you want?" he inquired.

She replied, "I want your identification seal, your cord, and the walking stick you are carrying." So Judah gave these items to her. She then let him sleep with her, and she became pregnant. Afterward she went home, took off her veil, and put on her widow's clothing as usual.

GENESIS 38:7-19

We learned in our previous lesson that Judah chose to marry a forbidden Canaanite girl. He also chose a Canaanite bride for his son. This young bride's name was Tamar.

Tamar means "date palm." Date palms were highly valued trees, not only for their delicious fruit but also for their stately beauty and ability to thrive in the desert climate. This teenage bride was not named so by coincidence.

What do we learn about Tamar from the preceding passage?

What kind of choices (if any) did Tamar have?

When she went back to her father's house, do you think she expected to ever return to Judah's household? Why or why not?

At what point do you think Tamar realized there would not be another wedding?

Tamar decided to take things into her own hands. She may have thought, *Judah is a widower and free to take another wife. Certainly his own seed would secure his promise to me of offspring.* Or, *I'll take only what is promised to me!*

When Tamar set her plans in motion, she changed out of her widow's clothing. What did she do at the end of the passage? What is significant about this? (If you need a hint, consider the following: Did she stop any other men who were on their way to the sheep-shearing? Did she stay on with Judah? Did she continue to play the harlot? Did she brag about her actions?)

This woman of action now waits. She waits to see if Judah will accept her solution to their dilemma. She waits to see if she will be the one to build Judah's household. She waits to see the God of Judah judge between Judah and herself!

Read the following passage:

> People may be pure in their own eyes, but the Lord examines their motives. PROVERBS 16:2

What does Proverbs 16:2 say about people's opinion of themselves?

FIND GOD'S WAYS FOR YOU

Up to this point in Tamar's life she had been abused, used, abandoned, and forgotten. Have you ever been treated unfairly? How have you handled broken promises?

In what ways do you identify with Tamar?

Have you ever run ahead of God and tried to fix things yourself? If so, what was the outcome?

STOP AND PONDER

> Jesus said, "Come to me, all of you who are weary and carry heavy burdens, and I will give you rest. Take my yoke upon you. Let me teach you, because I am humble and gentle, and you will find rest for your souls. For my yoke fits perfectly, and the burden I give you is light."
>
> MATTHEW 11:28-30

Pause to consider the burden you are carrying. Will you do as Tamar did and try to handle it yourself? Or will you let Jesus take your grief, disillusionment, unfair treatment, and disappointments? Take on Jesus' "yoke." Allow Him to give you a hope and a future.

exposure

SEEK GOD'S WORD FOR TRUTH
Read the following passage:

> About three months later, word reached Judah that
> Tamar, his daughter-in-law, was pregnant as a result of
> prostitution. "Bring her out and burn her!" Judah
> shouted.
>
> But as they were taking her out to kill her, she sent this
> message to her father-in-law: "The man who owns this
> identification seal and walking stick is the father of my
> child. Do you recognize them?"
>
> Judah admitted that they were his and said, "She is
> more in the right than I am, because I didn't keep my
> promise to let her marry my son Shelah." But Judah never
> slept with Tamar again. GENESIS 38:24-26

When Judah heard that Tamar was with child, what was his response? Was this a private proclamation or a public one?

Judah may have thought, *This will let me off the hook with my promise to her of Shelah!* He may also have thought, *Who will blame me for getting rid of Tamar?* What was Tamar's response to the death sentence her father-in-law demanded?

Why do you think Tamar asked Judah a question rather than making a proclamation? What does this reveal about her character?

A choice was now laid before Judah. He could once again run and hide, ignoring the truth; or he could, at last, do what was right. According to the passage we just read, what was Judah's response?

What does Judah's response reveal about his character?

Read the following passage:

> People who cover over their sins will not prosper. But if they confess and forsake them, they will receive mercy.
>
> PROVERBS 28:13

A heart that has confessed and forsaken sin will be declared righteous by God through Christ Jesus. Both Tamar and Judah found God's forgiveness and saw Him work out His good purposes through their lives. Only God can bring blessing from disaster, deceit, and disillusionment. Only God knows the heart of a person.

Read the following passages:

> In due season the time of Tamar's delivery arrived, and she had twin sons. As they were being born, one of them reached out his hand, and the midwife tied a scarlet thread around the wrist of the child who appeared first, saying, "This one came out first." But then he drew back his hand, and the other baby was actually the first to be born. "What!" the midwife exclaimed. "How did you break out first?" And ever after, he was called Perez. Then the baby with the scarlet thread on his wrist was born, and he was named Zerah.
>
> GENESIS 38:27-30

> "For I know the plans I have for you," says the Lord. "They are plans for good and not for disaster, to give you a future and a hope."
>
> JEREMIAH 29:11

Judah was the father of Perez and Zerah (their mother was Tamar). Perez was the father of Hezron. Hezron was the father of Ram. MATTHEW 1:3

Tamar had hoped for a son. What did God do for her?

Judah had hoped for an heir. What did God do for him?

FIND GOD'S WAYS FOR YOU

Have you ever been privately confronted about something you did or said that was wrong? If so, how did it make you feel?

Have you ever been openly rebuked, embarrassed, or corrected? How did you respond?

When Tamar was openly confronted, she presented the truth (as she knew it). When Judah was confronted with the truth, he repented. He had run away from both his family and his faith. God used the consequences of his choices to bring about repentance and restoration. In your experiences of being confronted with something you did wrong, what were the consequences? If you had it to do over again, how might you respond differently?

STOP AND PONDER

> Let us go right into the presence of God, with true hearts fully trusting him. For our evil consciences have been sprinkled with Christ's blood to make us clean, and our bodies have been washed with pure water.   HEBREWS 10:22

> God saved you by his special favor when you believed. And you can't take credit for this; it is a gift from God. Salvation is not a reward for the good things we have done, so none of us can boast about it.   EPHESIANS 2:8-9

How is God drawing you?

SEEK GOD'S WORD FOR TRUTH

From our brief study, we have seen how circumstances offer
choices to be made in life. Those choices can lead to destruction
and disillusionment or to restoration and a productive life. In
review, look back at the Bible passage in "Setting the Scene"
on pages ix–xii. What kind of man was Judah then?

The following passage is lengthy, but it's important for learning
the end of Judah's story. It took place many years after the incident
with Tamar, when Judah and his brothers appeared before their
long-lost brother Joseph. Joseph had risen to a position of great
authority in Egypt. He recognized his evil brothers and decided to
put them to a test to see whether they had changed. The brothers
did not know that the man wielding the power of life or death over
them was, in fact, Joseph.

> When his brothers were ready to leave, Joseph gave these
> instructions to the man in charge of his household: "Fill

each of their sacks with as much grain as they can carry, and put each man's money back into his sack. Then put my personal silver cup at the top of the youngest brother's sack, along with his grain money." So the household manager did as he was told.

The brothers were up at dawn and set out on their journey with their loaded donkeys. But when they were barely out of the city, Joseph said to his household manager, "Chase after them and stop them. Ask them, 'Why have you repaid an act of kindness with such evil? What do you mean by stealing my master's personal silver drinking cup, which he uses to predict the future? What a wicked thing you have done!'"

So the man caught up with them and spoke to them in the way he had been instructed. "What are you talking about?" the brothers responded. "What kind of people do you think we are, that you accuse us of such a terrible thing? Didn't we bring back the money we found in our sacks? Why would we steal silver or gold from your master's house? If you find his cup with any one of us, let that one die. And all the rest of us will be your master's slaves forever."

"Fair enough," the man replied, "except that only the one who stole it will be a slave. The rest of you may go free."

They quickly took their sacks from the backs of their donkeys and opened them. Joseph's servant began searching the oldest brother's sack, going on down the line to the youngest. The cup was found in Benjamin's sack! At this, they tore their clothing in despair, loaded the donkeys again, and returned to the city. Joseph was still at home when Judah and his brothers arrived, and they fell to the ground before him.

"What were you trying to do?" Joseph demanded. "Didn't you know that a man such as I would know who stole it?"

And Judah said, "Oh, my lord, what can we say to you? How can we plead? How can we prove our innocence? God is punishing us for our sins. My lord, we have all returned to be your slaves—we and our brother who had your cup in his sack."

"No," Joseph said. "Only the man who stole the cup will be my slave. The rest of you may go home to your father."

Then Judah stepped forward and said, "My lord, let me say just this one word to you. Be patient with me for a moment, for I know you could have me killed in an instant, as though you were Pharaoh himself.

"You asked us, my lord, if we had a father or a brother. We said, 'Yes, we have a father, an old man, and a child of his old age, his youngest son. His brother is dead, and he alone is left of his mother's children, and his father loves him very much.' And you said to us, 'Bring him here so I can see him.' But we said to you, 'My lord, the boy cannot leave his father, for his father would die.' But you told us, 'You may not see me again unless your youngest brother is with you.' So we returned to our father and told him what you had said. And when he said, 'Go back again and buy us a little food,' we replied, 'We can't unless you let our youngest brother go with us. We won't be allowed to see the man in charge of the grain unless our youngest brother is with us.' Then my father said to us, 'You know that my wife had two sons, and that one of them went away and never returned—doubtless torn to pieces by some wild animal. I have never seen him since. If you take away his brother from me, too, and any harm comes to him, you would bring my gray head down to the grave in deep sorrow.'

"And now, my lord, I cannot go back to my father without the boy. Our father's life is bound up in the boy's life. When he sees that the boy is not with us, our father will die. We will be responsible for bringing his gray head down to the grave in sorrow. My lord, I made a pledge to my father that I would take care of the boy. I told him, 'If I don't bring him back to you, I will bear the blame forever.' Please, my lord, let me stay here as a slave instead of the boy, and let the boy return with his brothers. For how can I return to my father if the boy is not with me? I cannot bear to see what this would do to him."

GENESIS 44:1-34

What do we learn about Judah from this account?

In what ways had Judah changed?

Read the following Bible passage, which tells the end of the story:

Joseph could stand it no longer. "Out, all of you!" he cried out to his attendants. He wanted to be alone with his brothers when he told them who he was. Then he broke down and wept aloud. His sobs could be heard throughout the palace, and the news was quickly carried to Pharaoh's palace.

"I am Joseph!" he said to his brothers. "Is my father still alive?" But his brothers were speechless! They were stunned to realize that Joseph was standing there in front of them. "Come over here," he said. So they came closer.

And he said again, "I am Joseph, your brother whom you sold into Egypt. But don't be angry with yourselves that you did this to me, for God did it. He sent me here ahead of you to preserve your lives. These two years of famine will grow to seven, during which there will be neither plowing nor harvest. God has sent me here to keep you and your families alive so that you will become a great nation. Yes, it was God who sent me here, not you! And he has made me a counselor to Pharaoh—manager of his entire household and ruler over all Egypt.

"Hurry, return to my father and tell him, 'This is what your son Joseph says: God has made me master over all the land of Egypt. Come down to me right away! You will live in the land of Goshen so you can be near me with all your children and grandchildren, your flocks and herds, and all that you have. I will take care of you there, for there are still five years of famine ahead of us. Otherwise you and your household will come to utter poverty.'"

Then Joseph said, "You can see for yourselves, and so can my brother Benjamin, that I really am Joseph! Tell my father how I am honored here in Egypt. Tell him about everything you have seen, and bring him to me quickly." Weeping with joy, he embraced Benjamin, and Benjamin also began to weep. Then Joseph kissed each of his brothers and wept over them, and then they began talking freely with him. GENESIS 45:1-15

Clearly, Joseph was deeply moved by Judah's plea. What was Joseph's response to Judah and the rest of his brothers?

God had made provision for the entire family. He had spared Joseph's life and given him a position of great authority. He had brought restoration to Judah and his brothers.

Reread the following passage about Tamar:

> Then Judah told Tamar, his daughter-in-law, not to marry again at that time but to return to her parents' home. She was to remain a widow until his youngest son, Shelah, was old enough to marry her. (But Judah didn't really intend to do this because he was afraid Shelah would also die, like his two brothers.) So Tamar went home to her parents.
>
> GENESIS 38:11

At that point, what kind of future did Tamar have to look forward to?

Now read the following Bible passage, written many years later:

> And may the Lord give you descendants by this young woman who will be like those of our ancestor Perez, the son of Tamar and Judah.
>
> RUTH 4:12

How was Tamar remembered by her descendants?

Tamar had her hopes and plans, but God had bigger plans. He gave her twin sons, who became the forebears of the tribe of

Judah. Ultimately, the Messiah—the promised Savior of the world—came from that tribe.

FIND GOD'S WAYS FOR YOU
Just as God worked in the lives of Judah and Tamar, He works in our lives today. In what ways is God revealing Himself to you?

As you have worked through these lessons, what changes do you sense you may need to make in your life?

Who holds your future? According to Jeremiah 29:11 (see page 151), who is offering you a future?

STOP AND PONDER

> For God so loved the world that he gave his only Son, so that everyone who believes in him will not perish but have eternal life. God did not send his Son into the world to condemn it, but to save it.
> There is no judgment awaiting those who trust him.

> But those who do not trust him have already been judged
> for not believing in the only Son of God.   JOHN 3:16-18

Are you ready for the future? If you have not given your life to Jesus Christ, you can do so right now. All you need to do is say a simple prayer. Confess that you are a sinner and that you desire to turn around, and invite Jesus Christ to come into your heart as your Lord and Savior. When you belong to Jesus, you can be assured of an eternal future and hope for today.

Choose life!

SEEK GOD'S WORD FOR TRUTH

As we've already seen, the story of Tamar does not end with the birth of her twin sons. We can trace Judah and Tamar throughout the Bible. The following passages are a few examples of the future God had in store for them:

> "I am Joseph!" he said to his brothers. "Is my father still alive?" But his brothers were speechless! They were stunned to realize that Joseph was standing there in front of them. "Come over here," he said. So they came closer. And he said again, "I am Joseph, your brother whom you sold into Egypt. But don't be angry with yourselves that you did this to me, for God did it. He sent me here ahead of you to preserve your lives. These two years of famine will grow to seven, during which there will be neither plowing nor harvest. God has sent me here to keep you and your families alive so that you will become a great

nation. Yes, it was God who sent me here, not you! And he
has made me a counselor to Pharaoh—manager of his
entire household and ruler over all Egypt.

"Hurry, return to my father and tell him, 'This is what
your son Joseph says: God has made me master over all the
land of Egypt. Come down to me right away! You will live
in the land of Goshen so you can be near me with all your
children and grandchildren, your flocks and herds, and all
that you have.'"   GENESIS 45:3-10

How did Joseph feel about Judah?

In the following passage, Judah receives a blessing from his father,
Jacob (also known as Israel). What are the key elements of this
blessing?

Judah, your brothers will praise you. You will defeat your
enemies. All your relatives will bow before you. Judah is a
young lion that has finished eating its prey. Like a lion he
crouches and lies down; like a lioness—who will dare to
rouse him? The scepter will not depart from Judah, nor
the ruler's staff from his descendants, until the coming of
the one to whom it belongs, the one whom all nations will
obey. He ties his foal to a grapevine, the colt of his donkey
to a choice vine. He washes his clothes in wine because his
harvest is so plentiful. His eyes are darker than wine, and
his teeth are whiter than milk.   GENESIS 49:8-12

Read the following passage. How was Moses' blessing different from Jacob's blessing?

> Moses said this about the tribe of Judah: "O Lord, hear the cry of Judah and bring them again to their people. Give them strength to defend their cause; help them against their enemies!"
>
> DEUTERONOMY 33:7

In the following passage, who chooses Judah?

> Then the Lord rose up as though waking from sleep, like a mighty man aroused from a drunken stupor. He routed his enemies and sent them to eternal shame. But he rejected Joseph's descendants; he did not choose the tribe of Ephraim. He chose instead the tribe of Judah, Mount Zion, which he loved.
>
> PSALM 78:65-68

Genesis 38—the story of Tamar and Judah, upon which *Unveiled* is based—can be seen as a celebration of the father and mother of a tribe. Tamar was held in great respect. Her actions were carried out with the sole intention of having a child to carry on the family. God saw her heart and gave her children. God also knew Judah's heart and provided a way for him to be restored to his family, as well as his descendants, to carry on his name. Ultimately, God used the line of Judah to give the world the Messiah. The Messiah is often referred to as the Lion of Judah. Jesus is Messiah!

FIND GOD'S WAYS FOR YOU

Is there someone with whom you need to make amends,
as Judah did?

Like Tamar, we all have hopes and dreams for the future. What
kinds of things do you hope for?

How do you want to be remembered?

STOP AND PONDER

"My thoughts are completely different from yours," says
the Lord. "And my ways are far beyond anything you
could imagine. For just as the heavens are higher than the
earth, so are my ways higher than your ways and my
thoughts higher than your thoughts.

"The rain and snow come down from the heavens and
stay on the ground to water the earth. They cause the
grain to grow, producing seed for the farmer and bread for
the hungry. It is the same with my word. I send it out, and

it always produces fruit. It will accomplish all I want it to, and it will prosper everywhere I send it. You will live in joy and peace. The mountains and hills will burst into song, and the trees of the field will clap their hands! Where once there were thorns, cypress trees will grow. Where briers grew, myrtles will sprout up. This miracle will bring great honor to the Lord's name; it will be an everlasting sign of his power and love."   ISAIAH 55:8-13

May God's Word always produce the fruit of obedience and accomplish much in you.

THIS is a record of the ancestors of Jesus the Messiah, a descendant of King David and of Abraham:

Abraham was the father of Isaac.
Isaac was the father of Jacob.
Jacob was the father of Judah and his brothers.
Judah was the father of Perez and Zerah (their mother was **Tamar**).
Perez was the father of Hezron.
Hezron was the father of Ram.
Ram was the father of Amminadab.
Amminadab was the father of Nahshon.
Nahshon was the father of Salmon.
Salmon was the father of Boaz (his mother was **Rahab**).
Boaz was the father of Obed (his mother was **Ruth**).
Obed was the father of Jesse.
Jesse was the father of King David.
David was the father of Solomon (his mother was **Bathsheba,** the widow of Uriah).

Solomon was the father of Rehoboam.
Rehoboam was the father of Abijah.
Abijah was the father of Asa.
Asa was the father of Jehoshaphat.
Jehoshaphat was the father of Jehoram.
Jehoram was the father of Uzziah.
Uzziah was the father of Jotham.
Jotham was the father of Ahaz.
Ahaz was the father of Hezekiah.
Hezekiah was the father of Manasseh.
Manasseh was the father of Amon.
Amon was the father of Josiah.
Josiah was the father of Jehoiachin and his brothers (born
    at the time of the exile to Babylon).
After the Babylonian exile:
Jehoiachin was the father of Shealtiel.
Shealtiel was the father of Zerubbabel.
Zerubbabel was the father of Abiud.
Abiud was the father of Eliakim.
Eliakim was the father of Azor.
Azor was the father of Zadok.
Zadok was the father of Akim.
Akim was the father of Eliud.
Eliud was the father of Eleazar.
Eleazar was the father of Matthan.
Matthan was the father of Jacob.
Jacob was the father of Joseph, the husband of Mary.
Mary gave birth to Jesus, who is called the Messiah.

MATTHEW 1:1-16

a b o u t   t h e   a u t h o r

FRANCINE RIVERS has been writing for more than twenty years. From 1976 to 1985 she had a successful writing career in the general market and won numerous awards. After becoming a born-again Christian in 1986, Francine wrote *Redeeming Love* as her statement of faith.

Since then, Francine has published numerous books in the CBA market and has continued to win both industry acclaim and reader loyalty. Her novel *The Last Sin Eater* won the ECPA Gold Medallion, and three of her books have won the prestigious Romance Writers of America Rita Award.

Francine says she uses her writing to draw closer to the Lord, that through her work she might worship and praise Jesus for all he has done and is doing in her life.

The Mark of the Lion trilogy: *A Voice in the Wind, An Echo in the Darkness,* and *As Sure As the Dawn*

The Scarlet Thread

The Atonement Child

Redeeming Love

The Last Sin Eater

Leota's Garden

The Shoe Box

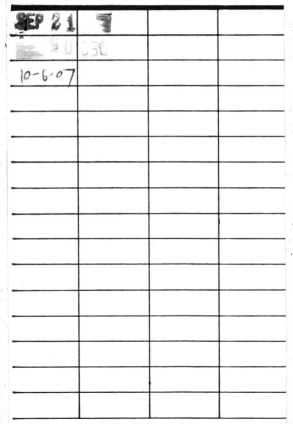

DATE DUE

SEP 21			
9 0 030			
10-6-07			